Praise for Hannah Alexander

"Alexander is great at drawing the reader
into her storyline and keeping them hooked
until the resolution of the plot."
–*Christian Retailing* on *Sacred Trust*

"The strength of emotion packs a powerful punch,
and the suspense sits on the edge of a knifepoint...
Hideaway is an absolute must read for everyone."
–*Romantic Reviews Today*

Praise for Jill Elizabeth Nelson

"This book has a well-developed plot and
an excellent mystery that will keep you guessing
until the final pages."
–*RT Book Reviews* on *Legacy of Lies*

"A wonderful mystery with a great heroine
keeps the reader guessing."
–*RT Book Reviews* on *Witness to Murder*

HANNAH ALEXANDER

is the pseudonym of husband-and-wife writing team Cheryl and Mel Hodde (pronounced "Hoddee"). When they first met, Mel had just begun his new job as an E.R. doctor in Cheryl's hometown, and Cheryl was working on a novel. Cheryl's matchmaking pastor set them up on an unexpected blind date at a local restaurant. Surprised by the sneak attack, Cheryl blurted the first thing that occurred to her, "You're a doctor? Could you help me paralyze someone?" Mel was shocked. "Only temporarily, of course," she explained when she saw his expression. "And only fictitiously. I'm writing a novel."

They began brainstorming immediately. Eighteen months later they were married, and the novels they set in fictitious Ozark towns began to sell. The first novel in the Hideaway series won the prestigious Christy award for Best Romance in 2004.

JILL ELIZABETH NELSON

writes what she likes to read—faith-based tales of adventure seasoned with romance. By day she operates as housing manager for a seniors' apartment complex. By night she turns into a wild and crazy writer who can hardly wait to jot down all the exciting things her characters are telling her, so she can share them with her readers. More about Jill and her books can be found at www.jillelizabethnelson.com. She and her husband live in rural Minnesota, surrounded by the woods and prairie and their four grown children who have settled nearby.

HANNAH ALEXANDER

JILL ELIZABETH NELSON

of SEASON of DANGER

Love Inspired

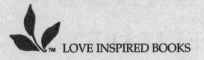

LOVE INSPIRED BOOKS

Recycling programs
for this product may
not exist in your area.

ISBN-13: 978-0-373-44469-4

SEASON OF DANGER

Copyright © 2011 by Harlequin Books S.A.

The publisher acknowledges the copyright holders
of the individual works as follows:

SILENT NIGHT, DEADLY NIGHT
Copyright © 2011 by Hannah Alexander

MISTLETOE MAYHEM
Copyright © 2011 by Jill Elizabeth Nelson

www.LoveInspiredBooks.com

Printed in U.S.A.

CONTENTS

SILENT NIGHT, DEADLY NIGHT   7
Hannah Alexander

MISTLETOE MAYHEM   119
Jill Elizabeth Nelson

SILENT NIGHT, DEADLY NIGHT

Hannah Alexander

This story is dedicated to the fabulous editors and staff of Love Inspired, who work hard to reach the world with tales of hope and encouragement.

My brothers, as believers in our glorious
Lord Jesus Christ, don't show favoritism.
Suppose a man comes into your meeting wearing
a gold ring and fine clothes, and a poor man in
shabby clothes also comes in. If you show special
attention to the man wearing fine clothes and say,
"Here's a good seat for you," but say to the
poor man, "You stand there" or "Sit on the floor
by my feet," have you not discriminated among
yourselves and become judges with evil thoughts?
—*James* 2:1–4

ONE

At eleven-thirty on Tuesday night, two hours after the canned Santa Claus music had gone blessedly silent out on the street, a squeak, which sounded like rubber-sole shoes on tile, reached Tess Vance from the hallway outside her locked office door. She heard footsteps…almost rushed…sneaky.

She straightened from her computer keyboard and frowned. She knew the cadence of her brother's swift pace. Gerard Vance had the legs of a giraffe. He could cover the length of the hallway in less than ten steps, and he didn't walk as if he was sneaking anywhere. Neither did Sean Torrance, who also had his office up here. Besides those two men, Tess was the only person who had a key to the admin offices.

Tess stacked several sheets of information that needed to be entered into the data system. She was preparing to stand up and stretch her aching back when she heard another echo of footsteps, rushed as before. Her heartbeat rocked through her body.

Was her imagination working overtime with the rest of her? She glanced at the phone on the corner of her desk, unreasonably terrified of being alone right now.

A homeless woman, Carlotta, who had come to the mission more than once for food and a place to sleep, had been found dead two weeks ago, not far from here. It appeared she'd been ill and exposed to the elements. No one suspected foul play except Tess…and possibly Sean and Gerard, though neither of them had told her what they thought.

Tess couldn't get that awful announcement from her mind. It had been related on the local Channel 11 as a brief aside, as if Carlotta didn't matter as much as someone with money and an address.

One channel that had treated her death as the tragic event it was had been KSFJ, 106.1 FM, the radio station that had been owned and managed by the Torrance family for the past two decades. After Sean inherited the station and took over management three years ago, he'd brought with him a whole new level of popularity—and compassion.

Despite Tess's anxiety—or perhaps because of it—she settled her thoughts on Sean, who had the ability to calm her tension with nothing more than a look, a gentle word, a touch on her hand. He was the person who had helped Tess in the past eight months, since joining Gerard in the work at this mission, to convince local churches to organize a system of volunteerism for the rescue missions and soup kitchens in the region.

Sean had been a godsend to Gerard, Tess and their older brother, Hans, and to the hundreds of homeless in multiple cities who benefited from his organizational skills. Everyone who knew him benefited from his big heart. But Tess couldn't help feeling she benefited the most.

Tess felt the tension in her body ease. In contrast to her brother's Nordic blond, rugged good looks, Sean had hair as dark as the night sea and eyes the color of midnight surf. He did share Gerard's size and strength and thoughtful consideration toward others—despite his wicked sense of humor when he and Gerard teased Tess.

She considered calling one of the two men. Just in case. She suddenly felt reluctant to wander these hallways alone tonight.

She reached for the phone and allowed her hand to hover over it but quickly chastised herself for being jittery. She'd worked many late nights alone in the mission with less crew than they had tonight. There was nothing to worry about. She glanced over her shoulder toward the barred window that overlooked the street and saw nothing but a reflection of those protective bars. No movement. Maybe one of the children had somehow slipped upstairs, had become lost trying to sneak back for more of the banana pudding cake that was Sean's special—and secret—recipe.

But the kitchen was downstairs, not up here.

Something felt different tonight. Maybe it was the measure of activity that had kicked into high gear here at the mission because Christmas was here in a little over two weeks, or maybe it was the lateness of the hour. Gerard had been forced to rely more and more on volunteer staff since Tess arrived nine months ago—he and Hans were saving for their next move in the rescue mission project. They wanted to establish a rehabilitation center.

With the exception of Sean, who was a tireless worker, the most experienced volunteers wanted to spend more hours shopping, decorating and prepping for Christmas parties. The Vance Rescue Mission had been left with seasonal help, folks with good hearts who knew little about the work involved.

Of course, Gerard's ground rules helped a lot—when an able adult refused to work, that adult didn't eat, so those in need of food knew they might have the opportunity to earn their keep here. Gerard believed this rule was not only helpful for the mission, but it engendered self-respect for those who worked for their meals.

Another footstep echoed out in the hallway—the sound of hesitation, only one step, then silence.

Tess closed her eyes and waited. She knew she was still suffering from stress disorder after her fiancé's death in March. The sense of horror continued to follow her nine months after Tanner Jackson was intentionally run down and killed. She was jumpy, startled easily and seldom felt at peace in her surroundings.

Her hand continued to hover. One place she did feel at peace was in Sean's presence. And why wouldn't she? He was six foot four and weighed probably 220, all muscle. Was she simply looking for an excuse to see him one more time tonight?

Until this past March, Tess had never been a nervous person. She had dealt with all kinds of people in her marketing agency. She could handle anyone from self-absorbed diva performers to angry authors whose novels didn't sell as well as they'd hoped to belligerent employees who thought they had a right to company finances. A few times in the past, she'd been forced to ruffle feathers. She still desperately needed to know whose feathers she'd ruffled enough to get Tanner killed.

Again, the sound of footsteps reached her, rushed, staccato. Someone was running in the hallway. The steps came closer. The locked knob rattled, and then something rammed the door.

Tess opened her mouth to scream, fists clenching as she braced for someone to break through. But she pressed her lips together, took a deep breath, willed herself to remain silent as she squeezed her eyes tightly shut.

She could handle this; she didn't need to go running to Gerard or Sean. She reached into the top drawer of her desk and grabbed the pepper mace, slammed the drawer shut.

The echo of diminishing footsteps told her she was already too late, but she reached the door, slung it open and glanced each direction along the hallway. A shadow on the far window to her left was all she saw of her intruder, and then it was gone.

She paused, frustrated, frightened and ashamed. It could still be a rambunctious little boy who had found his way up here. Perhaps someone had left the door unlocked? Who would've been able to ram her door so hard that the impact still rattled in her brain? Not a little boy. Teenager plying a little mischief?

Something on the polished tile floor caught her attention at the bend of the corridor to her right, as if someone had tracked—what was it, straw?—from outside. Something from a manger scene?

Though Tess had always been nearly as courageous as her

brother, courage had failed her lately. Gerard would worry if he knew, so for the past nine months she'd kept her trepidation to herself as much as possible.

The straw on the floor hadn't been here when she'd come upstairs three hours ago. She'd heard no one while she was doing data entry and planning a new strategy for promotion.

She wasn't a clean freak, but she stepped into the hallway to investigate. She was bending over to pick up the litter when a footstep from behind startled her so badly she had to strangle a scream. She held the mace up and pivoted.

It was Sean. His hulking shoulders seemed to expand to the width of the hallway. She went weak and nearly collapsed. "Do you know how close you came to sneezing pepper?"

Sean Torrance had the most melodious laughter she'd ever heard. "Janitorial volunteers didn't show up tonight?"

She didn't return his smile.

"Sorry," he said, still chuckling. "A little jittery, aren't you? Poorly done Christmas music does that to me, too, though not quite to the point of wanting to mace someone."

She narrowed her eyes at him, raising one brow in threat.

Sean forced himself to stop laughing. Since he and Gerard had first been assigned as partners in the Corpus Christi police force ten years ago, he'd been undeniably drawn to Gerard's younger half sister. She was like a fiery angel with hair and eyes the color of shiny onyx. She'd been able to make him smile when nothing and no one else could, especially these past months.

"You're just so doggone cute when you glare like that," Sean told Tess.

Her dark eyes flared, and he was tempted to taunt her a little—tell her outright that she should stop trying to deny her attraction to him, because he wasn't buying it. But he knew better. Tess had been different ever since Tanner's death. He knew she still blamed herself, though she never talked about it.

"Cruel," she said to him. "That was cruel." Her eyes darkened further as she pushed past the fear that seemed to cling to her. She'd been startled. He could see that now.

"I know. Sorry. What've you got?" he asked, nodding at the straw and whatever else she held in her hand.

"Did you hear the noise out here a moment ago?" she asked.

"Yeah. Thought it was you, so I stepped out for some company, and lo and behold, there you were, showing me a whole 'nother…um…side of yourself." He bounced his eyebrows in an attempt at a leer.

"I meant, before I came out."

The leer vanished. "I take it you weren't the one running, banging around out here. I mean, remember the time we had that infestation of mice, and you chased—"

"Not mice. Not this time."

"Tess, what happened?" He was suddenly a cop again.

She held up the straw. "The running, banging on the door, it was someone else. Someone tried to break—and I mean literally break—into my office. Who could have gotten up here? Where's Gerard?"

Sean felt himself go cold inside. He reached beneath his coat for his sidearm.

"No." She touched his arm, shaking her head. "It may be nothing. No need for guns."

"You're sure?"

She hesitated, took a deep breath, and Sean knew she was much more spooked than she wanted to let on.

"Gerard's been gone for hours," Sean told her. He reached for the material in her hand, sniffed it, wrinkled his nose. "Manure and mud. Someone come up here from a feedlot?"

She shrugged.

"Did you lock behind you when you came upstairs?" he asked.

"I always do. You?"

"Sure did." Gerard had told Sean he'd purchased this building in this district of town because he knew this was where they would find the most people in need, but he also knew that calling it a mission didn't protect this place from danger more than any other place of business in the area. The secondhand store they operated in the connecting building kept money, and this time of year they brought in a lot.

"How long have you been here?" Tess asked.

"Half the day. I'm working on year-end accounts for the station, and I can't get anything done there. Too many interruptions." Not that he didn't have plenty of interruptions here... and distractions just down the hallway. The beautiful lady's presence could be very distracting.

Tess took a deep breath, let it out slowly. She flexed her shoulders and met Sean's gaze again, as if looking at him made her feel safer.

He stepped closer. "Maybe we could share an office for a while, at least until things slow down after the holidays."

She hesitated for a moment, obviously thinking about it, but then she shook her head. "You just want the office with the bathroom in it," she said, as if she, too, was teasing. But he could hear the tremor in her voice.

"Not true." He followed her as she stepped back into her small office. "There's no room for two desks in here. You'd have to move in with me."

"Not happening. I like my private bathroom."

"We could change the locks to our upstairs sanctuary."

"Good idea. Tomorrow?"

"First thing in the morning." He glanced again at the clump of strange evidence in his hand. "Got a plastic bag?" he asked.

She reached into the set of trays on the wall and pulled out a self-sealing envelope. "That's the best I can do."

He dropped the straw, mud and manure into the envelope, took it from her, sealed it and set it on the corner of her desk. He then went into the small half bath and washed his hands. She joined him. No telling where that stuff came from.

Though Sean and Gerard had both left the police force more than three years ago—Gerard to join their brother in an extremely successful start-up, a green-manufacturing plant to help support this mission, and Sean to take over his family-owned radio station—they both retained the instincts of policemen.

He believed that was one reason Tess felt safe working here for the time being, living in the back wing of Gerard's house, never too far away from either Sean or Gerard. For the first time in her adult life, this past year she'd allowed herself to be protected by her older brothers. And Sean.

The men had made a pact to keep watch over her and protect her at any cost. That wasn't always easy, because Tess was independent to the point of arrogance at times. Sean wasn't going to tell her that. At least not at this point of their non-relationship.

Sean had seen pictures of Gerard and Hans's mother, and of Tess's. Lawrence Vance's first wife was of Swedish descent, blond hair nearly white, and the men favored their mother. Tess's mother, Maria—who had named her daughter Theresa and was the only one who still called her that—had moved to Austin from Mexico City six months after Lawrence's first wife was killed in a car wreck. Maria had met Lawrence in church and had fallen in love with his two children. After thirty-three years of joyful matrimony, the loving couple continued to live west of Austin. Maria was the only mother Gerard had ever known.

Tess stretched her hands and arms as she walked to the window of her office and closed the blinds. "What a day this has been. My back aches, my head hurts, and my neck is as stiff as a starched, new rope. Breakfast was a long time ago."

"I thought I saw a long line outside the soup kitchen this evening," he said.

"Gerard told me they fed nearly twice as many as usual. A hundred and fifteen at last count, with many more teens and children than usual. I wonder if the other kitchens are as overwhelmed."

"Maybe we're serving the best food today."

"Why do people get laid off at Christmas?"

Sean shook his head sadly. "It's below freezing outside to-night. Did we have enough room for overnighters?"

"There were three men with no place to go. Gerard couldn't find a bed for them anywhere in the city."

"Don't tell me," Sean said. "He put them in the subbase-ment."

"With blankets and pillows."

"Against regulations, of course."

"You'd do the same. Gerard can't turn them out to freeze."

Sean leaned against the edge of Tess's desk. "He's always been a soft touch, but don't you dare tell him I said that."

Her dark eyes slid over him with apparent appreciation as he spoke. "Beneath his tough-guy exterior is a heart of spun honey."

"It runs in the family," Sean said.

"Tough-guy exterior?"

"You never could take a compliment."

A light gleamed in her eyes as she silently acknowledged his words. "Guess that spun honey rubs off on his friends, too." She picked up the envelope and handed it to Sean. "Glad I didn't mace you."

"I've been maced before. I'd have lived through it."

"At least there were enough cots for the women and children tonight," she said. "But I'm not sure how much longer this can go on. We need larger facilities. Can you get this straw checked out? See where it came from?"

"Will do. We've still got friends connected to the force."

Tess glanced at the clock and gave a sigh of obvious frus-tration. "Midnight."

"What time are you due back tomorrow?" Sean asked.

"Early. I have to supervise breakfast prep."

"Gerard can't do that?"

"He's got a meeting in Houston first thing in the morning. Court case."

"Then it's time for you to wrap things up." Sean tucked the envelope into his shirt pocket and reached for Tess's purse and jacket. "Out you go. And don't come in at five. I can do it; you get some extra sleep. I've seen how many hours you put in here."

Tess gazed into his eyes and made him think of things he knew were impossible at the moment. She was still grieving. She looked worn down. She had looked that way since before Tanner's death—had probably begun to have those circles under her gorgeous eyes about the time the first threatening note showed up under her door.

"I have more to do tonight," she said. "If I don't get it done now, I'll just have to—"

He took her by the shoulders and guided her toward the door. "You're done. Joni and Mamie will be more than happy to help you tomorrow."

"Mamie has a job interview."

"That won't take all day. We've got extra help coming in tomorrow from a new church start-up, so take advantage of it. We need it. Mamie can enter data, and Joni can file for you tomorrow."

The homeless population of the past years had exploded with whole families out on the street after foreclosures on homes, repossession of vehicles, loss of jobs. Those who were accustomed to work were so appreciative of the help they received that they freely gave of their time serving in the kitchen, filing and entering data, housekeeping, working in the mission store. This four-level double building utilized a lot of volunteers.

Sisters Joni and Mamie Park had owned their own storefront antique shop, with a large apartment upstairs, until this past summer when fire broke out and destroyed everything they owned except for their delivery van.

When they started coming to the soup kitchen for meals, Sean had discovered they were sleeping in their van and cleaning up at the public bathrooms at the beach while looking for work. In the months before the fire, their business had declined to the point they'd been unable to pay for insurance. The timing had been horrible for them.

Gerard's dream was to create more jobs and set up a career rehab center somewhere far from here. He would most likely make that happen. Sean wanted to be a part of that by staying behind and helping Tess manage the mission while her brother was off in search of a new place of promise.

"Okay," Tess said. "I think after ten-thirty at night from now on, we're going to have to put bells on our toes." She preceded Sean from her office and waited for him to lock it.

"I don't care what you say. No bells. Don't we hear enough bells around here lately?"

She followed him to his office door. "Don't tell me Gerard's stuck with two Scrooges here at the mission."

"It's easy to feel overwhelmed by the crowds during Christmas season." He pulled a thick briefcase from his office, locked up and held an arm out, indicating that she should follow him.

"I can't stop thinking about that pistol you carry," she said.

"You have pepper mace, I have the protection I'm most comfortable with." Sean didn't mention that Gerard also carried a concealed weapon. Gerard had insisted his key personnel carry protection on these dangerous streets, not only to protect themselves, but to protect the helpless ones who were stuck outside at the mercy of too many deadbeats.

"In a way, my brother has expanded your police force in Corpus Christi by adding a private security division," Tess said.

"Who else is going to protect them? He protects his own, and that encompasses everyone in need."

"Face it, my brother's a hero. Is it any wonder I've seen our pretty doctor spending so much time with him lately?" Tess followed Sean down the stairs.

Sean smiled, but he wouldn't mention that even Dr. Megan Bradley, who was working at the mission to pay off her med school loans, also carried a concealed weapon at Gerard's behest. She took it with her when she and Tess had a girls' day out.

"Or perhaps I should say, it isn't any wonder why Gerard can't seem to stay away from the clinic." Tess cast a side glance at Sean. "She could win an international beauty contest."

"I don't think he sees that." Pretty as Megan was, she held none of the mystique for Sean that Tess Vance held.

Tess groaned. "He's a man, isn't he?"

"I think he enjoys her company, but I've honestly never heard him remark on her physical attributes. You know your brother, he always looks at the heart first."

Tess hesitated at the doorway in the rear of the kitchen, where several of the late workers, mostly Hispanic volunteers from the church three blocks from the mission, were sweeping the floor, emptying trash and having their dinner of leftover chili.

"All right!" Tess said, grinning at last. "The special is chili, and I haven't eaten since my late breakfast." She cocked an eyebrow at Sean. "How about it, Torrance? Gerard's not here to challenge me right now, and Hans is always stuck up in Austin, watching over that manufacturing plant. Which of us can take it the hottest?"

"Hey, Señorita Vance," called Angel Mancillas, the pastor from the church. "You're welcome to join us, as always, and I brought your favorite habaneras sauce my Sandra makes."

Tess rubbed her hands together and grinned at Sean. "If I remember correctly, you like hot stuff."

He held her gaze. "Love it." He pulled a chair out for her, then joined her, and for the next thirty minutes, she seemed to relax and think about something besides the footsteps in the upper hallway. If only he could always make her feel so safe.

TWO

The telephone awakened Tess long after dawn. She got a blurry look at the clock—it was eight—before she grabbed her cell phone. Caller ID showed it was the Vance Mission Clinic.

"What's up?" she asked, pushing Gerard's affectionate Dobermans from the bed. When had Romper and Roxie climbed under the covers with her?

"Tess, this is Megan. Are you okay?"

At the urgency in the doctor's tone, Tess sat up and swung her legs to the side. "I'm fine. Why? What's happened? Is Gerard—"

"Your brother's perfectly healthy, long ago landed at Houston, but we appear to be having some kind of illness among the regulars. Since I'm not sure Gerard's out of court yet, I decided not to call him about this."

"What kind of illness?"

"Gastrointestinal symptoms. We've had six come in so far, and they're feeling pretty rough. I'm trying to decide if it's a virus of some kind, or if we've had some food go bad."

"We've never had food poisoning in our kitchen. How many of them ate at the mission yesterday?"

"All six."

"I ate breakfast and dinner there, even challenged Sean to a hot-sauce competition. Have you seen him?"

"He was in the kitchen cooking just now, told me to call you, but he's feeling as healthy as always."

"So am I, and I ate a sample of everything. Could it be a stomach virus?"

"It's always possible, but that wouldn't hit everyone all at once like this. Only food poisoning would hit everyone so suddenly, and these are some of our regulars. All of them had their flu shots this year. I saw to it."

"We never have tainted food. We watch that closely."

"I haven't had time to take extensive histories. It's possible they've all eaten elsewhere."

"That's most likely, since I'm not feeling a thing."

"You're healthier than most homeless people, Tess. And it's likely you didn't eat the same batch of food. These all ate early last night."

"Are you taking samples?"

"Yes, and I'm getting bogged down."

"I'll be there in twenty minutes."

"Uh-oh. Here comes another one."

"I'll call in some backup. Maybe some of our volunteer medical personnel will be off duty today."

"Thanks," Megan said. "I think I'll have Mamie drive to the pharmacy for more supplies."

"No, just call in your order and get Mamie to the clinic to help you. She mentioned the other day she was a volunteer medical aide in high school. I can pick up the order on my way."

After hanging up, Tess pulled on a fresh pair of jeans and a sweater as the dogs fought each other for her attention. She kissed Roxie and Romper on their foreheads, scratched their ears and smiled at Roxie's groan of contentment.

"Sorry, kids, gotta run. You want out?"

Of course, they did. She unlocked the door and watched them race each other through the doorway and out into the huge fenced yard, then, despite her watchdogs on alert, she locked the door again. How long since she'd felt safe when she was alone?

And the stress over the mission illnesses was making her

worse. Often, people from participating churches would bring side dishes or desserts to help feed the hungry, but yesterday all the food had come from the Vance Mission kitchen, and they tested their raw meats and produce often. It had always been an obsession of Gerard's to make sure the people he fed received wholesome, healthy food.

But Megan had said more than once that those living on the street were more susceptible to any illness that came along. They had weakened immune systems from exposure and often a history of poor lifestyle choices.

Despite the attempt to reassure herself, Tess felt the stress growing as she brushed her teeth and combed her hair. She grabbed her jacket and keys and rushed into the garage, where she parked her Cooper. As the garage door opened, she pressed the first phone number on her cell for nursing help.

She called herself all kinds of a fool on the drive to town. This was not her fault. Not her responsibility. She did not cause anyone to get sick…she couldn't have caused this in any way… could she?

No. But she couldn't get the sound of those footsteps out of her head from last night and the fear that, even in the absence of more of the threats she'd begun to receive ten months ago, someone out there still wanted to hurt her by hurting those she cared about.

By the time she reached the pharmacy, she had promises from a nurse and two techs to meet her at the mission. She drove to the pick-up window and exchanged friendly insults with Troy, the tech on duty, who had asked her out at least once a month since she'd arrived in Corpus Christi.

"Sounds like you've got an outbreak at the mission," Troy commented as he heaved two big bags out the window to her. "Flu season has hit hard."

"You've had a lot of orders like this?"

He nodded.

"But these patients had their flu shots."

He raised his bushy eyebrows in surprise. "That's weird.

We've always got our rogue viruses, of course, but this year's inoculations seemed to be hittin' the bull's-eye."

She thanked him and drove to the mission as the tension knotted multiple times in her stomach.

Sean held an emesis basin for a man in his fifties who'd never answered to any name but Stud. Three more people had walked into the clinic after Sean traded kitchen duties for clinic duties at Megan's request, and all of them looked miserable.

Megan had drawn blood, given eight shots so far for nausea and handed out multiple little envelopes of pills to help with the stomach cramps. She told Sean she wanted to do a blood draw on Stud as soon as she could get to him; he had a chronic alcohol history, and that could make him prone to electrolyte imbalances. She'd managed to collect some stool samples on the others and remarked three times in the past five minutes that she hoped Tess arrived soon.

And Tess did, looking harassed and pale, carrying in two large bags imprinted with the local pharmacy logo. Soon after she arrived, an RN who volunteered at the clinic two Saturdays a month walked in the door, pulling off her coat and wrapping her stethoscope around her neck.

"Feeling better, Stud?" Sean asked his patient softly.

The man nodded and used the paper towel Sean handed him. "Need to clean up."

"Go get a toothbrush and toothpaste in one of the bathrooms down the hall and then go into the men's dorm. Lie down and rest until the doctor can get to you for your blood test."

Stud shook his head. "Got a job helping a man fix a fence a couple of miles out of town. I need the money."

"At least rest until we have a better idea about what you've got. If it's infectious, nobody's going to thank you for showing up. Give me a telephone number, and I'll call to let him know you didn't bug out on him, but you need to be here for Dr. Bradley to check you out."

"Got no number. How would I call? Really, I'm feeling better."

"You have the man's name? If the doc can get a diagnosis from your blood, you could be helping out a lot of sick people."

Stud gave in, and Sean hunted down the phone number of Stud's temporary employer and left the message. When he hung up, he caught sight of Tess, her large, beautiful eyes as haunted as they'd been yesterday when he'd found her in the corridor. The smudges beneath her lower eyelids seemed to have deepened overnight, and she'd lost the typical glow in her complexion.

"How are you feeling?" she asked, stepping over to him.

"Good. Did you sleep last night?"

"Off and on. I had a nasty wake-up call."

"Tess, I can't believe this is food poisoning." He was just glad he had a strong stomach. He'd never signed up for clinic duty, and for a few moments, he'd thought he might have to hunt down his own emesis basin.

"Me neither, unless they all ate something elsewhere. Or unless it wasn't the food itself that poisoned them."

As soon as she spoke the words, she closed her eyes and bit her lower lip, long strands of her black hair falling over her forehead.

"So, what you're saying," he said softly enough that the others couldn't hear, "is that you aren't ruling out poisoning of some kind."

Her shoulders slumped, and she nodded. "That's what I'm saying."

He stood up and took her arm, led her from the clinic proper for a moment. "You're trembling."

She put a hand over his. Hers was icy. "I'm sorry. Leftover post-traumatic stress disorder, I know. Also, I can't get past Carlotta's death two weeks ago."

"That was ruled a natural death."

"Easy for the authorities to do that when she's homeless with no family."

"You're obsessing over it."

"So sue me."

"What you're really anxious about is that Tanner's killer is still out there," Sean said, guessing at the direction of her thoughts.

Tess raised her hand from his and pulled her fingers through her hair. "I know it's not all about me. But those notes, Sean, I can't stop thinking about them, reading them, trying to figure out who might have sent them to me and what kind of person that might have been."

"Vindictive."

"Of course, but how vindictive?"

"You think enough to poison homeless people?"

"I'm thinking all kinds of things right now."

"And you're driving yourself crazy in the process."

"I'm not crazy," she snapped.

"You know that's not what I'm saying."

"Whoever wrote those notes threatened to hurt me or those I loved."

"I know. I still have copies, and I've reread them a few times myself." The paper and print had both been impossible to trace because they were so common. Sean knew how frustrated Tess had been when the police gave up searching for Tanner's killer. Some of the officers had even suggested that Tess was imagining the attack, despite the solid evidence of tire rubber on the asphalt. As one officer had pointed out, that could have been done at any time.

"Something about the wording leads me to believe the writer was female," Sean said.

Tess slowly raised her gaze to his. "You really are still on the case."

Sean didn't mention that her ex-cop brother was, as well. "Someone did die, Tess. Nothing's happened since. Whoever wanted to get revenge on you got it with Tanner's death."

"So you're saying I'm being unreasonable to think that same someone might try again."

"I'm saying you need to stop torturing yourself."

"What do you mean?"

"With guilt. You've been overwhelmed with it all these months."

"He was crossing the street to see me when he was hit. I'm going to feel some guilt about that, Sean. It's a human emotion."

"You weren't the driver."

She rubbed her neck and turned away. "It wouldn't be hard for someone to track me down with my last name matching the name of this mission, and someone did try to break down my door last night. You heard the noise yourself."

Sean had known she'd been more shaken up by that intruder than she would admit to him. He'd thought she was doing better, and he had told Gerard to keep watch on the house last night.

Not only did Gerard have thoroughly vetted help on his small ranch, but he had a state-of-the-art alarm system and two protective Dobermans who lived indoors, adored Tess and would never let a stranger close to her. Romper, the male, would barely even let Sean close when he drove out to the house for a visit, though both dogs were affectionate with him, as well.

He put an arm around her and walked her farther from the clinic entrance and into the larger rooms toward the back. "There's no reason to think a simple outbreak of food poisoning could have anything to do with Tanner's death. It wouldn't match the M.O. Poison would be a whole new profile."

"Not necessarily. Didn't you once tell me that sometimes a killer simply uses whatever's at hand?"

Sean paused. "You know what we've discussed about Tanner's reputation before," he said quietly.

She gave him a querulous look.

"He was a rising country music star," Sean said. "He had the bad-boy persona. You told me yourself that before the two of you became an item, he left a trail of broken hearts. That's why you kept your engagement quiet. He also got into a few fistfights at some late-night establishments."

"Staged. I told him not to do that, but he wanted that kind of publicity."

"The multiple romances—often at one time—weren't staged, were they?"

"You think he might have dated a killer?"

"At least he finally had the sense to know a good woman when he saw her," Sean said, rubbing his knuckles over her cheek. "You're an amazing woman, Tess."

She swallowed daintily and looked up at him, her olive complexion deepening a shade. She didn't say anything, just looked at him.

A woman walked past them toward the connecting second-hand store and drop-off facility, and the moment was gone.

Sean straightened. "But Tanner also aligned himself with unsavory people of both sexes, if you ask me."

"Been reading the rags?"

"Let's just say I did a few background checks."

"While I was engaged to Tanner?"

He nodded. For a moment, he couldn't bring himself to reveal what he'd discovered.

She tilted her head, obviously intrigued. "You never told me this stuff."

"You weren't the one who made enemies—he was."

"The crime wasn't solved, Sean."

"An entertainer doesn't behave the way he did without making enemies. You're not being fair to yourself. I don't like to accuse a man who isn't here to defend himself, and I certainly don't want to hurt you, Tess, but Tanner lived a self-indulgent life and he didn't give two cents for who he hurt."

"He cared about me."

"His actions didn't back up his words or the ring he put on your finger."

"You're saying he dated another woman when he was engaged to me?"

For some reason, she didn't sound surprised. Had she guessed? She also didn't sound devastated. "Women. Plural." Sean studied her expression, confused. "I'm sorry, Gerard and I had decided not to burden you with some of the information we dug up about him, but in my opinion, the guilt is proving to be more destructive to you than a broken heart."

But he saw no signs of a broken heart. What he saw was a brief whisper of, what—simple sadness?

"There's no danger of that," she said, confirming his suspicion. Intriguing.

More people walked past them. The drop-off and the store were getting busier.

"Want to go upstairs?" Sean asked. "Maybe we should discuss this further."

"Megan needs help."

"She has a very efficient nurse, two more techs just walked in to help Mamie, and you brought her the supplies she needs. I'm not saying there is any more danger from Tanner's killer, but if there is we should see if we can get to the bottom of it." Or at least divert her attention from the break-in and dial down the stress a few notches.

Tess hesitated, then sighed and nodded. "Don't you dare tell Gerard I'm doing this."

"Doing what? Struggling because you see people suffering?"

"Don't tell him I'm being paranoid. Again."

At least she was admitting it. Sean pulled two keys from his pocket, gave Tess one and used the other to unlock the door to the administration offices. "Changed the locks myself at first light this morning."

She took hers from him, took his hand, looked up at him. "Thank you, Sean. How can you be so many places at once?" Her voice was suddenly soft, tremulous. Some light had returned to her eyes.

"Believe me, I wish I could be."

"You're always there when I need you. You always have been."

His skin felt the warmth of her skin, and he couldn't resist losing himself, for just a moment, in that vulnerable, dark gaze. "Ever think that's a touch from God?" he asked.

She smiled, then nodded. "I think that's exactly what it is."

It seemed an appropriate time to reassure her. He pressed a light kiss on the top of her head. "Don't want to miss my calling."

Her smile widened. She pulled out her key ring. As they went up the steps, she switched the new key for the old one on her ring, and Sean watched her steps for her. He was being overprotective, and he knew it. She'd pick up on it soon if she hadn't already, but doggone it if she hadn't settled over his heart like moist, rich chocolate frosting on a dried-up cake.

He unlocked his door and drew her inside. His office was the largest in Admin, with extra chairs. This was where they held their meetings, and this was where he or Gerard interviewed potential employees. Gerard also insisted on background checks on those volunteers who might be working with the homeless for a long period of time. He was protective of his people, and he'd grown especially so since Tanner's death. Sean suspected that Gerard also worried that there might be another attempt to hurt Tess.

"Have you heard anything about the straw and manure we found last night?" Tess asked.

"Yep. At first glance they decided it was straw, manure and mud. Sorry. Hard to be any more specific yet, but it's most likely from a nearby barn lot. They're running more tests at my request."

"Did Megan send out any blood and stool samples yet?"

"She did. Mamie had Joni take some of them to the lab to get started," Sean told her. "They'll check for Norwalk virus and rotavirus since there are sick children—and salmonella, Shigella, and E-coli, as well as the usual intestinal parasites. Those are all the scientific words I can remember."

"What about the food?"

"Volunteers are scouring through the stores of food we have right now." As he talked, he was aware of the warmth of her beside him, the smell of her hair, and his hands still felt the touch of hers.

"They won't find anything off in our kitchen. No one will," Tess said.

"All seems fresh so far. Dates are good, freezers have worked perfectly, and if anything, the cooks overcook the food. The stomach pains seem to have hit the Hispanics harder for some reason."

"You think this might be a racial thing?"

"Megan doesn't see a reason for racial profiling. There just happened to be more Hispanic people in the line yesterday and Monday because Angel and Sandra did a great job of bringing in their church members to help, and word spread in their community."

"I called Gerard on my way here and left a message," Tess said. "None of this makes sense, though. If it isn't a virus, and we're sure it isn't our food, then what?"

Sean allowed the silence to return as he watched Tess nibble at her lower lip. She was really obsessing over this. "Tess, we can't go around second-guessing every action we take simply because we might accidentally make it convenient for some psychopath to commit murder."

She sighed, resting her chin in her cupped hands.

"Just don't jump to any conclusions yet, okay?" Sean bumped shoulders with her. "Hey. Okay?"

She leaned back, as if to leave some space between them. "A psychopath did kill Tanner, but that psychopath also sent the threatening notes to me, not to him."

"You showed them to the police, to us, to Tanner. You're off the hook completely."

Tess held Sean's gaze, looked down at her hands. "Remember last Christmas? When Mom and Dad took that cruise on the Mediterranean, and the rest of us came to Gerard's for Christmas dinner?"

Sean hesitated. That was a sudden and uncomfortable change of subject. "Not willingly."

"I'm sorry. I promise I don't mean to bring up bad memories, I'm just trying to make a point."

Sean took a deep breath and braced himself. He had brought a date—a sales rep from Houston—simply because he had known Tess would be there with Tanner, and he was a little too sensitive about that. His date turned out to be the biggest mistake of his life. If only he'd never met Kari Ann. He'd allowed things to go way too far. They'd used no protection. He didn't find out she was pregnant until she'd already decided to abort.

Tess placed a hand on Sean's arm. She was no longer ice-cold. "Kari Ann made her choices, too. You tried to stop her. I was here, remember? I saw how hard you tried."

He took another slow, deep breath to control the fury-riddled frustration at the situation he'd helped create—and the grief over the abortion of his offspring. He'd have gladly raised his baby alone, if only Kari Ann had been willing to bring that helpless, beloved child to term.

All that rage and pain had brought him to his knees and to Christ, with Gerard's support.

But today, Tess was the one in need of strength.

"I'm sorry," he said. "What were you going to tell me about last Christmas?"

"Only that something changed in me during those days. I realized that I'd left my faith behind when I left my family and went out to make my own life."

"You were always ethical."

"Oh, I always tried hard to be ethical in my business dealings, but I made my own plans without seeking God's plans for me."

"You're talking about Tanner?"

She nodded. "Somewhere along the way, God stopped being

my reason for living, and Tanner turned my head—much like he did all his female fans. I mean, the man had the looks, the personality and the moves, you know?"

"Um, not really."

"Okay, no, you wouldn't. But that voice alone could melt a person."

Sean felt suddenly restless. He did not want to think about the effect Tanner had on Tess.

"But when I spent time at the mission last Christmas," she continued, "I saw what Gerard and Hans were doing. It made an impact. I slowly began to realize I was missing it all, and that my relationship with Tanner Jackson might not be the right one for me."

"But you continued your engagement." That, too, had been frustrating to Sean, especially after he realized, just watching Tess with Tanner that week during Christmas at the Vance ranch, that the two didn't belong together.

She hadn't realized Tanner's depraved mind, his selfish disregard for anyone who didn't serve his needs. Tanner hadn't understood—if he cared at all—the kind of man Tess needed in her life. It simply was not him.

"It's one thing to make a life-changing discovery about yourself," she said, "but it's another thing altogether to break it off with the person you've been planning to spend your life with."

"You need to learn to listen to your heart."

"I continued to believe we could make it work, despite the rumors and some of the sly innuendoes on gossip TV and trash magazines. I talked to him about my faith and how it had been reaffirmed, how I had finally realized that serving God wasn't just following a set of rules, but knowing Him and putting Him first."

"And?"

"He didn't like the change in me."

"So he was jealous of God?"

Tess shrugged. "You could put it that way, I guess. We

pushed each other further and further away." She nibbled again on her lower lip. "He'd never been the person I tried to convince myself he was."

"You always like to believe the best about people." It was one of the things Sean loved about her.

"But here's the crux of the matter, Sean," Tess said. She leaned forward. "The night he died, I'd called him to come over. I had the ring in its original box, ready to give to him."

"What? You mean…you're saying you were breaking the engagement?" All Sean's memories of that time suddenly shifted sideways in an effort to contain this new information.

"Yes. I couldn't keep it up. I was holding the ring in my hand when I heard the gunning of an engine outside and then the squeal of rubber on the street." She closed her eyes.

"You don't have to relive it. I have everything memorized." She hadn't loved Tanner when he died. She was blaming herself for that?

She looked up at Sean sadly. "I still have nightmares about running out the door and seeing that car disappearing around the corner two blocks away. I still dream about the blood."

Sean was reaching out to cover her hands with his when his telephone rang. He glanced at Tess, pressed the speaker button and answered.

"This is Dr. Bradley," came a shaky voice over the speaker. "We've been coding Stud. He's asystole. Ambulance is on its way."

"Flatline!" Tess jumped up.

"We couldn't get him to respond to shock," Megan said.

Tess grabbed Sean's hands. "He's dying."

Sean caught her as she fell.

THREE

Tess floated through a dark tunnel, aware of nothing but the sound of a man's voice shouting in the far distance. She couldn't understand what he was saying and didn't know why he was shouting. Was it a warning? Or was he angry?

He fell silent, and she drifted until something cold and wet dripped onto her face. Then she felt herself being lifted.

Sounds finally smacked through her ears again: the thud of footsteps, hard breathing, other voices, doors opening and closing.

"Tess? Honey, wake up now. You're scaring me. Please open your eyes." It was Sean's deep voice, directly above her.

Light slid beneath her eyes, and she squinted up to find Sean carrying her into the clinic.

"Tess," he breathed. "Thank goodness." He laid her on a cot at the far end of the room from where paramedics and Megan stood around a supine man.

"I'm wet," Tess said.

Sean brushed her hair from her eyes, standing between Tess and the crowd around the cot across the clinic, where privacy curtains had been pushed back. "I splashed water on you to wake you."

"Stud?" She remembered.

Sean hesitated. "He didn't make it. Megan called medical control to see if they need to take his body to the hospital or have him taken to the morgue."

Megan rushed from the crowd to Tess's cot. "Tess Vance, when's the last time you ate anything?"

"About midnight."

Without pulling a curtain, Megan pressed her stethoscope over Tess's chest.

Tess breathed for her. "You okay?"

"Hush and let me listen."

"Your eyes are red, and your face is white as—"

"Tess." Firmly.

"Megan, relax. I was shocked to hear about Stud. That's all."

"Heart and breathing sound okay, despite the fact that you've suddenly turned into a chatterbox. I'll check your blood sugar."

"You don't have to do—"

Sean touched her shoulder. "Be good and listen to the doctor."

Megan pricked Tess's finger and read the number on the glucometer. "Seventy-nine. Not low. You fainted over the death of someone you don't know very well."

"PTSD, okay? I faint easily. Look, you already have your hands full, and you don't need me complicating matters." Tess glanced at Sean. At least he wasn't offering any unsolicited information the way Gerard would do if he were here.

"PTSD from what?" Megan asked. "Is there something you never told me in all those days at the beach and nights out on the town?"

Tess eased herself up slowly. "When I'm out for a good time, I want to laugh, not cry about the past."

The clinic phone rang. Sean paused to make sure Tess would be okay and then walked into Megan's tiny office cubicle to answer, obviously so Megan could continue to grill Tess.

"Have you seen a doctor about your fainting spells?" Megan asked.

"Nope. Can you take a guess about what caused Stud's death?"

"I wish I could. There'll have to be an autopsy. The coroner is sending a car." Megan turned and dismissed the paramedics.

They walked out, and in the distance, Tess could hear the doors of the ambulance close in a heavy thud as the crowd dispersed. Unfortunately, many of them ambled toward Tess. Strangers, some of them, from off the street. Not homeless, just morbidly curious. Disgusting. She felt herself tense up as she glanced at the body lying on a gurney, covered by a sheet. It hurt to think of quiet, struggling Stud being cut open and displayed for examination.

"When were you going to get around to telling me about the PTSD?" Megan asked softly, waving the others away. They didn't move far. People around here weren't typically shy.

Tess took an irritable breath. "I apologize for not telling you."

"Then tell me now."

Tess glared toward the curious onlookers, who continued to gawk. "Private conversation here, folks." Her voice was a little too confrontational, and she didn't care. At last, the final stragglers ambled out the doorway.

Tess waited, annoyed by nosy people the way she'd never before been annoyed by them. "My fiancé was murdered in March."

"What! I never heard that. No one told me anything."

"We didn't tell anyone. I didn't want word to spread that my fiancé was Tanner Jackson."

Megan's full lips parted. "The country singer? That Tanner Jackson?"

"Quiet, please." Tess glanced toward the entrance again. "He was a client of mine. We hit it off, fell in love, got engaged late last year. Tanner didn't want to risk the ire of all his adoring female fans, so we kept it private."

"Why am I not surprised?" Megan muttered. "You said he

was murdered. I heard it was an accident. How could murder not have been blazoned all over the radio and gossip columns?"

"Good cops, good friends, tight lips. I am a publicist by profession, you know."

Sean hung up the phone and turned back to them. "Gerard's on his way. It's going to be okay, Tess."

Tess swung her legs over the side of the cot. "Not even my superhuman brother can just walk into a room and snap his fingers and make everything bad go away."

"Dizzy?" Megan asked.

"I'm fine. How are the other patients?"

"They're sleeping in the dorms, with folks keeping close watch on them," Megan said. "Angel was called in a while ago, and he's in the men's dorm, Sandra is in the women's dorm, praying with those who are afraid, helping the nurse and techs as they work. A couple of the ill are from their church."

"So they aren't all undernourished homeless."

Megan shook her head. "And you said you ate a little of everything yesterday."

"That's right. I'll go help Sandra." Tess started to get up.

"You'll do no such thing," Megan said. "You will rest, as you should have been doing all along. If you don't stop pushing yourself so hard, I'm going to call in reinforcements."

Tess raised her eyebrows. "Yeah? Like who?"

"Mister Superhuman."

"You think he's going to make me behave?"

"Yep."

Megan stepped across the clinic to close the door.

Sean stepped from Megan's tiny office and sat down beside Tess on the cot, and she welcomed his sturdy presence. She needed his strength. She was also glad when Megan returned to them.

Dr. Megan Bradley had graduated second in her class at Kirksville Osteopathic in Missouri. She and Tess were nearly the same age, and both being professional single women, they tended to talk the same language, except for the second language Megan had learned in med school.

Since Tess had allowed Gerard to bully her into moving home with him and helping out at the mission after Tanner's death, she and Megan had become close. She'd helped Megan in the clinic many times, and they'd spent their few off hours together shopping or looking for the best seafood restaurants in town, or, as Megan said, walking along the beach.

Megan was understandably mystified about why Tess had never told her about Tanner's death, but Tess simply hated talking about that time in her life. She'd had too many nightmares, anyway, and she wanted those nightmares gone. Her arrival home with Gerard in March had met with no fanfare, no announcements.

Now Tess was sorry she hadn't even given Megan at least a warning before this morning's episode. After all, Megan had been working here when it all took place; they just hadn't known each other well.

"The good news," Sean said, patting Tess's shoulder, "is that no more sick people have come in for the past…what did you say, Megan? Thirty minutes?"

"More like forty-five. Betty arrived just a few moments ago, and she's helping Judy keep close watch over the patients in the dorms. I've completed all the tests and sent them to the lab."

Tess nodded. Both Judy and Betty were two of the best RNs in the area, with much knowledge and tender hearts. This mission was blessed with a lot of knowledgeable, caring people. Tess couldn't help silently asking herself if she belonged.

Sean leaned over and bumped shoulders with her. "I know that look."

She glanced up at him, and her eyes grew warm with moisture.

"Stop it," he said.

"Can't help it. I'm sad about Stud."

"You're somehow blaming yourself for this, like you blame

yourself for practically everything that goes wrong in the world. I think you've got control issues. You're not God."

Some of his words hit a sore spot. "When did you get the psychotherapy degree?" She knew her voice was a little sharp, but couldn't he let up on her a little? "It could be days before we find out what really happened to Stud. I don't feel good about not knowing."

Megan hovered over Tess. "I called the lab for a stat on all the fluids I sent them. Even if we don't get a quick answer from the autopsy, the lab staff is great, with good people to work with, and I've updated them. They know a lot of lives could be dependent on their work."

"In other words, we could find out what happened at any time," Sean said.

"I'm just waiting for the call."

"People don't often die from food poisoning," Tess said.

"Not food poisoning alone," Megan said. "But we know Stud had problems."

"Alcohol," Sean said. "Speed, too."

"Really?" Tess asked.

Sean shrugged. "From what little I've deciphered from a couple of our conversations, he occasionally got so down and depressed that when he came into extra money, he would combine alcohol with meth just to escape his life for a while."

Tess remembered the nights Gerard had been forced to ban Stud from sleeping in the dorm because of his altered level of consciousness and the danger that could cause for the other men in the dorm.

"I don't know how Gerard does it," Megan said softly.

Tess knew exactly what she meant. "He's a strong man. He and Hans have always had hearts for the suffering—even those who seemed to bring it on themselves."

"So do you, Tess," Sean said. "And Megan."

"And Sean." Megan grinned up at him.

"Okay, enough mutual admiration," Tess said dryly. "We're

all saints and angels. So why do we do what we do? I know why I'm here. I'm hiding from life. What about you two?"

"Same here," Sean said.

"Really?" Megan said. "Because I thought it was to be close to—uh, well—I'm here to work off my school loans. So maybe we're not such saints, after all. What are our clients and patients doing here?"

"Who knows why Stud abused alcohol and drugs?" Sean asked. "In the eight months I've worked here, I've discovered a lot of people try to self-medicate for depression, grief, mental illness they can't afford to have treated."

"That's the real reason we're here," Tess said. "As Gerard has so often reminded me since he and Hans established this mission, this place is the poor man's treatment center. It's a mission not only to help feed the hungry and try to shelter them, but to share God's love with them in a way they may never have experienced before."

With a soft sigh, Megan paced across the clinic. Tess watched her. Megan had long, ginger-colored hair, delicate but exotic facial features, a tiny waist. Her movements were graceful and feminine, but those features belied the inner strength Tess had seen in her on more than one occasion. Unfortunately, in the eighteen months she had been here, Gerard had not managed to convince her of the truth of God's mercy, which they shared with those who came here for help. Though Tess had no doubt that Gerard and Megan were drawn by some kind of unseen connection, Tess was convinced Megan would fulfill her final six months of duty and move on without anything being done to encourage a deepening of the relationship.

That saddened Tess. But then, everything seemed to sadden Tess these days.

She glanced again at Stud's sheeted form and reached for Sean's arm. Without a word, he put it around her, and she leaned into him, soaking up his warmth and strength. Sean had been such a good friend for such a long time. He was like another brother.

Only he wasn't. Not at all. She straightened and pulled away as Gerard entered the clinic.

There was something about Tess's brother that drew people the moment he entered a room. There was a power about him that his attractively craggy features and his pale blond hair and blue eyes did not explain. Like Sean, he was built like a wrestling champion. There was an energy that seemed to emanate from him.

Tess got up from the cot and walked into her brother's arms. "I'm so sorry about Stud. I know you worried a lot about him."

Gerard squeezed her tightly and kissed her on top of the head, much like Sean had done. "You doing okay, kiddo?"

Tess nodded, still soaking up some of her brother's strength from his closeness. "Have you told Hans?"

"I called him on my way here. Look, I just contacted the coroner, and the van is coming to get Stud. Tess, why don't you and Sean take a drive? Sean was up extra early and could use a break, and you don't need to be around right now. Megan and I can handle this."

"How long before the coroner arrives?" Tess stepped from her brother's arms at last.

"Maybe ten to twenty minutes."

"In that case, Megan, could we talk for a few minutes privately?"

"You mean so you can finally fill me in on those holes you've left out of your mysterious past year?"

"Pretty much."

"Lead on. I love mysteries."

Sean watched Tess lead Megan up the stairs to Admin and then turned back to Gerard, who stood over Stud, head bowed. At last, in the silence, Sean had a chance to grieve. Gerard wasn't the only one who'd spent quite a bit of time with the older man. When Stud was sober, he could entertain the children, charm the ladies and have all the men laughing over dinner. He wasn't a mean drunk, just sad. He'd cried a lot.

A hand fell on Sean's shoulder, and he looked up to find Gerard watching him. "I never promised this job would be easy."

Sean shook his head. "The worthwhile ones seldom are."

"There are good days. We help a lot of people here, Sean, and you're a big part of that."

"So is Tess, but I'm afraid it's taking its toll on her. She fainted when Megan called us about Stud."

Gerard closed his eyes. "I'm sure she asked you not to tell me that."

"I respect her wishes, but she didn't get a chance to ask this time."

"So, when are you going to convince her that Tanner was never meant to be the love of her life?" Gerard asked.

"You mean you haven't already told her that a dozen times?"

"I didn't say you should tell her. I said you should convince her. Big difference. Besides, she never listens to me. You know our Tess."

"Oh, that's right. You're the grouchy bear."

"That's Hans. I'm just too bossy."

Sean chuckled. "How you three headstrong siblings managed to reach adulthood without mangling each other is still a mystery to me."

"Let me guess. She fainted because she's still afraid Tanner's killer is going to resurface. Death does that to her. Every time she hears about a death, she's suspicious it's another covered-up murder that didn't reach the ears of the media."

Sean didn't reply. He didn't have to. Tess had no idea how well her brother understood her. Instead of saying a word, Sean reached into his pocket and pulled out a key. He held it out for Gerard.

"What's this?"

"Changed the locks to Admin. Again."

"Why?"

"Someone got in, tracked some stuff into the hallway. It was too late to call you. Whoever it was tried to force Tess's office door open. Why she would think anyone would know that was her office…" Sean shrugged.

Gerard glanced again at Stud's shrouded figure. "She thinks there's a connection."

"But food poisoning?"

"What do you think?"

"As I pointed out to her, the M.O. isn't the same, but as she pointed out to me, a killer might not always use the same M.O."

"This isn't like Tess, you know. The paranoia, the fear, the guilt. I'm her brother. I know her. At heart, she's a warrior."

"Yeah, I know. That's what bothers me."

"Megan hasn't heard back from the lab yet, right?" Gerard asked.

"She gave them a lot of work."

Gerard picked up the phone and pressed a speed-dial number while Sean tidied the clinic and changed paper on some of the cots.

"Tess, put Megan on the phone for a minute, would you… Yeah, Megan, you haven't received any results from the lab about our fatality?" Gerard asked. "Would you call them while I hold on this line?"

Sean stepped to the wall of windows and stared out at the street. He remembered Megan talking about patients who would walk over and close the shades, not knowing that the windows were mirrored glass—no one could see in.

But he could see out fine, and as he and Gerard waited for any kind of report on Stud—or any other patients, for that matter—he watched the front entrance to the mission store. He recognized a blonde woman with a ponytail and glasses. She was part of the crowd in the clinic when Stud died, and she was noticeable because she carried a large leather carrier slung diagonally over her shoulder and she dressed a little more elegantly than most people who entered the doors of the sec-ondhand store.

What was someone like her doing at the mission? Obviously, she hadn't come as a volunteer. Sean knew her from somewhere. But where?

"Nothing?"

Gerard's voice distracted Sean, and when he looked toward the woman again, she was walking quickly down the street.

"Then I need you to request a toxicology panel. You've got them on hold? Good. Tell them how quickly we'll need it. Yeah, yesterday would've been nice." He gave further details, thanked her and hung up, then turned to Sean.

"You honestly think someone could have poisoned our people?" Sean asked.

"Tess seems to think it's possible. I think she suspected the death two weeks ago, though she never said anything to me about it."

"Yes, and you were just complaining about Tess's paranoia."

"I was also telling you that she isn't like this. When the probable has been ruled out, it's time to start looking for the improbable."

FOUR

"**I** have something to show you." Tess turned to Megan as soon as she finished on the phone. She sank into her chair and opened her filing drawer. She pulled out copies of the type-written notes that had begun the reign of terror over her life and shoved them across the desk to Megan. "These started coming to me in Austin late last February."

Megan read the first note aloud. "'You are a life destroyer. You're a vicious, selfish woman who deserves revenge, and I will enjoy seeing you brought down.' Tess, what is this?"

"At first I thought it was from one of Tanner's old girl-friends or even an obsessed fan who found out we were en-gaged."

"What did the police say?"

"I didn't say anything to them when I received this one. I figured if it wasn't a jealous woman, it could be an ugly busi-ness practice. The entertainment business can be cutthroat, so this could have been simple intimidation—a threat to do anything from slandering my agency to slashing my tires. No death threat there."

"If Tanner was murdered, why wasn't he the one who re-ceived these notes?"

"Gerard and Sean thought it might have been from some-one I'd crossed in the past. The only conflict that was serious enough to inspire something like this was when I discovered my second in command, Emil Mason, was embezzling money from the agency. I brought him up on charges, and he went to prison."

"Is he still there?"

"Yes, and the police—as well as Gerard and Sean—checked out his close contacts and cleared them."

Megan flipped the page and read the next note. "'There is no going back for you. There are no amends to make. I will be there to watch you and your loved ones suffer when you least expect it, and I will be proud of my handiwork.'" She shook her head. "My goodness, this person is psychotic!"

"Hello? Killer? What's not psychotic about that? That's the one that made me decide to bring the police in. I also talked to Gerard and Sean. Tanner didn't take it seriously."

"But this is personal against you. Wasn't he at least worried about you?"

"I began to wonder the same thing."

"How were the notes delivered?"

"Different places at different times. After the first note, which was slipped under my door at home, I had security cameras placed in my home and office. The second one was under my windshield wiper when I came out of the grocery store one Saturday."

Megan sucked in a hiss. "Someone stalked you."

"Which is what still frightens me. People come into the mission all day long. I wouldn't know if someone was stalking me."

"Did you get police protection?"

"They drove by my house more often at night, checked on me at work, but they couldn't do much."

"So Gerard moved in with you. That's when he was gone so much. I remember he had some local pastors help out in his absence."

"Gerard hung around a lot after the second note. When he didn't, either Hans or Sean took turns flying up to sit in my office, chauffeur me and sleep on my sofa."

"And Tanner? Didn't he ever do anything to protect you?"

"No, and that was what killed the engagement for me. Plus he hated my so-called 'missionary' views on physical relations before marriage."

"So, you weren't engaged to him when he was killed?"

"I was planning to break the engagement the night he was killed."

"That's what Sean meant about your guilty feelings. But he's right, you know. You can't control the world."

"I had my car in the shop for a week and had just gotten it back a couple of days before. When my brothers weren't around to chauffeur me, I drove Tanner's car, because he was on a tour bus. The night Tanner was run down, it was raining, and he was wearing a hooded jacket. Tanner and I were practically the same height. He was five-ten, I'm five-eight. Someone could easily have mistaken him for me."

"Despite all his faults, it's sad to see his life end so early."

Tess studied Megan's expression. "You sound as if you knew Tanner."

"We attended the same university in Columbia, Missouri."

"Aha! So I'm not the only one keeping secrets."

"He just didn't rate a mention."

"I always told myself that without the constant confusion of his parents' divorce and his high-profile life, Tanner Jackson was really just a sweet country boy."

Megan's gaze darted away. "Sorry, Tess. I didn't know him when he lived on the farm."

"And?"

"All I ever saw was a spoiled brat who once threw a fit when he was given the wrong sports car on his twenty-first birthday."

That sounded like the Tanner whom Tess had finally discovered beneath the facade. "Tanner threw a fit when he found out Sean was spending time with me, in spite of the fact I was receiving threats. Why didn't I see it sooner?"

"Oh, he could turn on all that Jackson charm, believe me." Megan leaned forward. "Face it, real men like the Vance men and Sean Torrance are rare as dinosaur eggs. I think they're the last of their breed."

"True."

"Gerard told me you worked at a nearby packing house for two years to pay for your first car when you were in high school," Megan said. "No taint of spoiled brat in you. What did you do when Tanner got mad about Sean?"

"I backed down, told the men I could take care of myself— fought mightily with all three of my protectors over it—and lost the fight. That was when Sean started helping out here from time to time, so Gerard could spend more time with me."

Megan gave a perceptive nod. "Tanner saw it."

"Saw what?"

Megan's eyes looked tired, but for a moment they glowed with humor. "Sorry to interrupt. Continue."

"It was also when I bought some mace. The day he was killed I'd received another note, this one taped to the door of my office. The security video showed only a slight figure in black in the wee morning hours. Couldn't even tell if it was male or female." She gestured to the final note Megan held.

Megan glanced at the two lines. "'You destroyed my life. Turnabout is fair play.'"

"Sean thinks a woman wrote these. The police and Gerard weren't sure."

"It really does read like the words of a jilted woman, Tess."

"You mean, a woman saying that if she couldn't have him, no one would? We all considered the same thing, but if that was the case, why didn't she ever warn me to stay away from Tanner? Ironically, since Tanner was coming to the house that night, Gerard flew home that day to take care of some things, so no one else was with me."

Megan leaned her elbows on the desk, her face going pale. "Maybe your stalker was watching for anyone—maybe the first vulnerable prospect? She could have gotten Gerard?"

"I thought about that, but Gerard's too intuitive. I don't

think he would have been caught like that." Tess smiled. "Though it's nice that you care so much."

"That happened in March. Why do you still feel as if you're in danger?"

"We had a trespasser up here late last night. It's the first time I've gotten my mace out since I came here." Tess described it.

"Gerard hasn't harassed you about using deadlier protection?" Megan asked.

"You mean a gun?"

"Can you shoot?"

"I used to compete with Gerard, until he joined the police force. I just know I wouldn't be able to use a gun against anyone."

"Not even if your life was threatened?"

"A gun's not a lot of good against a speeding car coming at you out of nowhere."

Megan reached beneath her lab coat. "It's not much good against illness, either." She pulled out a powerful .357 Magnum, short barrel, which fit in her hand. "This thing shoots like a dream, you know. Gerard made me start carrying. Especially when I'm with you."

A trickle of goose bumps climbed Tess's spine. "Gerard did that?"

"Last March. Didn't tell me why."

Tess closed her eyes and sighed. "You have a license to carry?"

"I do now. He's more worried about you than you think. I know you two are always trying to keep secrets from each other, but he's constantly watching out for you. So is Sean."

"I don't think I'm safe for my family and friends to be around."

"I think they can take care of themselves." Megan tapped her finger on her weapon. "I'm a pretty good shot. And Sean would die for you. You know that, don't you?"

Tess slumped against the window sill. Sean. She closed her eyes.

"I'm beginning to wonder why you were really going to break your engagement," Megan said. "If it was simply because you figured out Tanner was a jerk or if you realized you'd actually loved someone else all along."

Tess didn't meet Megan's gaze, because Megan was good at reading her by looking her in the eyes.

"Tanner could turn heads," Megan continued. "Sean, on the other hand, proved he was willing to put his life on the line for a woman engaged to another man."

"Because I was Gerard's sister. A friend. He's an ex-cop, Megan."

Megan shook her head. "You should've seen the fear in his eyes when he carried you downstairs this morning. I mean, I always saw the way he looked at you…actually, the way you two look at each other."

Tess attempted to stop the grin that insisted on spreading across her face. Didn't work.

Megan returned the grin. "I'm right, aren't I?"

"You're turning into a romantic."

"There was terror in his eyes when he laid you on that cot down there. Panic when he beckoned me to come to you and such relief when you sat up on your own."

"Sean's off limits for me."

"Why?"

"I thought I loved Tanner. I was crazy about him, until I wasn't."

"All that charisma can be overwhelming, even for a woman of your substance and discernment. You know Sean and have known him for years. Huge difference there." Megan sighed as she replaced her pistol in its holster. "If you'd told me you were dating Tanner, I could have saved you a lot of time. As for Sean—"

"Don't you get tired of carrying that around?" Tess asked.

"You mean my excellent insight into men? Never."

"Your gun."

"As Gerard told me, I'd feel worse if someone threatened one of my patients and I had no way to protect them. This is not the safest part of town, even without your worries about Tanner's killer."

Tess's phone buzzed. It was Gerard calling to let them know the morgue van had arrived for Stud's body.

"You stay up here until we get him loaded, Tess." Megan pressed her hand against Tess's shoulder. "You've had enough excitement for the morning. Try not to worry."

"I'll be fine, lots of work. I'll call Mamie and Joni to assist."

"Gerard wanted you to take a break with Sean."

"This is one time my big brother won't get what he wants."

Megan rolled her eyes as she turned to walk from the office. "When will you learn?"

When Megan emerged from the admin stairwell alone, Sean caught the door and went through it and up the stairs. He found Tess standing at the window near the very spot where she'd picked up the straw last night. She was staring out over the street below, and he caught a glimpse of her profile. So sad. Still so vulnerable. He wanted to wrap her in his arms and take her far away from here. But she was Tess. She thought she was strong and tough and independent, and he had to help her keep up that image, until she decided otherwise.

And yet, who was he to be her knight in shining armor? He wasn't even able to save his own child.

"Hey." He didn't want to startle her.

She turned. When she saw him, the sadness seemed to retreat. "Did I ever thank you for watching out for me after the second note?"

"You told Megan everything?"

She nodded, pushing her wavy, black hair from her neck as she turned and walked toward him. She had a stride that could enchant an army. "I did thank you, right?"

"You treated all of us to a three-hundred-dollar meal and offered to buy us all cars."

She laughed. He loved to see her laugh.

"Do you mind if I ask you something extremely personal?" she asked.

"About what?"

"Kari Ann."

Whoa. Nothing like getting to the point. "You can ask if you keep in mind that she was before—"

"I'm not playing the blame game, you know. And yes, I know Kari Ann happened before you finally listened to Gerard's preaching."

"Actually, that whole nightmare was why I finally did listen. And you never play the blame game. It's one of the…" He paused. This wasn't the time.

She raised her eyebrows.

He shook his head. He'd been about to say that it was one of the things he loved about her. One of the many, many things. "Ask away."

"Did you love her?"

The question didn't surprise him—leave it to Tess. It did disturb him, though. Now it was his turn to look out the window, but he didn't see the street or the small glimpse of the bay he could catch from here.

He saw the ugliness of his heart. He hadn't realized at the time that he was using Kari Ann to take his mind off Tess. He didn't deserve Tess. She deserved better.

"For a while, I convinced myself that, in time, I might learn to love her." How lame it sounded now.

"You stopped seeing her in early March."

Sean nodded.

"Did your duties guarding me cause problems between you?"

"Are you asking if Kari Ann was jealous? She always was, but I didn't tell her I was guarding you. We were keeping the whole thing quiet, remember?"

"Why did you stop seeing her?"

"Because I realized I would never love her the way..." He looked at Tess, and wanted to devour her dark-eyed beauty with his gaze. "The way a woman deserves to be loved." The way he had come to care for Tess after spending so much time with her, watching over her, driving her all over the city to meetings, lying awake on her sofa, wishing things were different between them. Wishing she wasn't in danger.

And yet, that time they'd spent together had solidified the powerful attraction he'd felt for so many years into honest, painful love. Painful for him, anyway.

"I can be a dunce with some things," Tess said.

"What things?"

"Relationships. Romance. Love."

"I don't think any of us really get it. I obviously didn't."

"I see a few happily married couples at church," Tess said. "Not all, but quite a few. My parents were happy. Hans and Linda were happy for twenty years. He still grieves her death. My choices haven't always been that great."

"How so?"

"You really think Tanner was such a prince?"

"He slipped into a different character when he was with you and let it drop when you were gone. Gerard did a slow burn for months."

"He did? He never said anything to me about that."

"I think your brother trusted you enough to figure things out for yourself. You were my example, Tess. Instead of jumping into a physical relationship with Tanner, you gave yourself time to discover what he was like, and you made the right decision. Very wise, Tess. Exactly what I would expect from you."

She perched on the window ledge and looked up at him. "You really do know how to make a girl feel better."

"Yeah, well, how are you supposed to see a person's identity when a guy hides that identity beneath charm?"

"You don't do that."

"What? You're saying I don't have charm?"

"You're just you, and that doesn't require extra charm."

He gave her a slow smile. "I think that was a compliment."

"Of the highest caliber."

What was it about this woman that could make him weak as a kitten in her presence? Or make him feel drunk on the finest wine? He wanted to take her in his arms and kiss her until he could no longer breathe.

She pushed away from the window sill and strolled along the hallway. "I used to think I could read people."

"So did I." He followed her. "With some people, I just know they are trustworthy. When Gerard and I were first partners in the police force, he was outspoken, what he said made sense, and he had follow-through. He proved himself to me."

"Well, okay, but this is my superhuman brother we're talking about. What about others?"

"You mean like you? Oh, yeah, I instinctively trusted you the moment I met you."

"Why?"

"You have a steady gaze, a firm handshake." Sean grinned at her. "You want me to help find you a man as trustworthy and true as your brother?"

Tess blinked up at him, and he felt the impact of her sudden attention on him. Her mysterious gaze traveled across the width of his shoulders and then rested on his face, his mouth.

He glanced out the window again, toward that small section of the bay. "Want to go on a walk? You've been working too hard, and Megan's worried about you."

"The whole world is worried about me lately."

"We could drive to the beach and feed the birds. You always love that."

"I don't know." She narrowed her eyes as if seriously concerned. "Are you still packing heat?"

"Always."

A grimace. "When will I be able to walk outside these doors

without someone having to protect me? I mean, really, even on a girls' day out?"

"I'm…uh…not a girl, and I'm not suggesting we shop for makeup or dresses."

"Sorry, I was thinking of a cute little .357 Megan carries."

"Come on, let's get out of the neighborhood for a while. Doctor's orders."

"And you know how well I take orders."

"Okay, doctor's urgent plea."

Tess paused and looked up at him. Her gaze softened. She reached up and brushed her fingers through his hair, let them trail down the side of his face to his chin while he tried hard to breathe normally.

"Okay," she said, dropping her hand away.

His breathing came easier, but he'd much rather feel her touch than have oxygen. It seemed to him that both were equally vital.

FIVE

Tess felt the tension ease from her neck muscles. She gazed out at the sun-rippled water as Sean turned his red Chevy truck onto a seashell drive and parked near the water. From here they overlooked Laguna Madre of the Intracoastal Waterway. No waves, only seabirds and an occasional fish. From where Sean parked, they could see no other people, no other cars, only ocean craft on the water. Tess knew he'd done that on purpose.

"Sixty degrees, faint gulf breeze," Sean said as he slid from the truck. "Hard to believe it dropped to thirty one night."

Tess had learned to wait for him to open the door for her when he was guarding her in Austin. By the time he had her door open, she had her shoes off and the wide legs of her jeans rolled up above her knees.

"Wish I'd brought shorts," she said.

"I said sixty, not eighty."

"Yeah, but the sunshine says at least seventy-five. Perfect weather." She slid from the seat and dug her bare feet into the rough sand, releasing more of her tension. "Better yet, I wish I'd brought my swimsuit. At least the walk will toughen up my feet."

Sean chuckled.

"I love the scent of the gulf." She strolled out to the edge of the water. A boat raced by, too far away for her to see the people onboard.

This was one of her favorite places, not a long drive from

the mission, so on those stressful days when she just had to get some fresh air, she could usually depend on this isolated stretch of beach being unpopulated.

Sean received a call on his cell while she walked slowly, digging her toes in the sand, trying not to eavesdrop. But there was nothing to hear. All he said was, "Yes. I see. Nothing at this point. Thank you."

In a couple of minutes, Sean joined her, similarly prepared for the water with bare feet and legs. But his gaze rested on the far horizon. The call had apparently not been a happy one.

"Why don't you turn off your cell and relax for a bit?" she asked.

He brought a plastic-wrapped loaf of bread from behind his back.

"Bird food!" she cried.

"Organic, made from sprouted grains and seeds. Not sure what sticks it together without any flour."

"That's because you're not a cook."

"I can cook."

"You cook eggs. You make sandwiches. Ever bake bread?"

"You're kidding. Don't you need a bakery for that?"

Tess rolled her gaze to the sky.

"This stuff has to be good for the birds, right?" Sean continued. "I know it's not seafood, but a change of pace is always nice. At least, the birds always seem to think so."

Tess wrapped an arm around his taut waist in an impulsive hug, then abruptly pulled away. "Well, the water isn't as warm as bathwater, but I bet it feels good. Want to see who's willing to get the wettest?" Without waiting for a reply, she splashed into water up to her calves.

When she turned back around, Sean was pulling open the bag of bread and tossing some bits to a couple of nearby gulls. She stayed in the water, scrunching her heels down into the sand and savoring the feel of the sun on her face. "How did you know I needed this?"

"Gerard's idea, remember?" Sean held a piece of crust up with his fingers and tempted a gull to take it from him.

"The sky's going to be gray and white with birds before long." Squeals and squawks echoed down the length of the beach.

"He knows you better than you think he does," Sean said.

"Gerard?"

"Yep. He believes in you, too."

She splashed more deeply into the water. "That's good to know."

"And he loves you very much."

She frowned at him. "Have Gerard and I had a fight I don't know about?"

"Nope."

"Then why do you seem to be trying to reconcile us?"

Sean joined her in the water and handed her a chunk of bread. "Is that what I'm doing?"

"I'm not sure what you're doing. Maybe trying to build up my ego a little, but not to worry, my ego's fine." She tore off a piece of crust and ate it. "Mmm, delicious."

"It has all kinds of seeds in it."

"When did you get it?"

"Yesterday. I had it in the truck." Sean took a bite. "You're right, it's good, even if it is healthy. Maybe we shouldn't be feeding it to the birds." He pulled off another chunk, and a gull grabbed it from his fingers before he could stick it in his mouth.

Tess laughed.

"Gerard guessed everything after he heard that you fainted today," Sean said.

Her grin died. "And who told him that?"

"You never told me not to tell him."

"You know, sometimes you're like a little boy. What kind of 'everything' did he guess?"

"The truth, Tess. That you're still struggling with the fallout from March. You heard, didn't you, that Gerard had Megan order a toxicology panel on the blood?"

"When?"

"You were with her upstairs when he called her."

"I left her when she got the call. She didn't tell me what it was about. So you're saying he thinks—"

"I'm saying your brother trusts your judgment."

Tess tore off several small pieces of bread and threw them in the air by the handful, and soon they were surrounded by a cloud of feathered friends, as she had predicted. She gave herself to the moment, though she knew she probably shouldn't be feeding the birds like this. It would turn them into beggars. Instead of hunting for their meals, they would be more likely to litter the beaches with their droppings and become a nuisance to tourists. She only indulged on special occasions.

"What are you thinking?" Sean asked.

"About nuisances and bird poop."

He stopped in the process of placing another bite of the thick, moist center of the bread into his mouth.

She laughed at the consternation on his face. He placed the bite between her parted lips instead. It was so delicious.

He moved closer to her, until she could see the reflection of the rippling water in his eyes and could hear the sound of his breathing over the squealing of the birds.

"I love it when you laugh," he said as she chewed and swallowed. He'd suddenly gone serious. "You don't do that nearly as much as you used to."

Before she could think, his lips were firm but gentle on hers, his warm arms coming around her, birds and bread forgotten. Problems at the mission forgotten. Sickness and murder disappeared from her mind as the calm assurance and strength of Sean's touch gave her a peace and a feeling of rightness she hadn't known in such a long, long time.

She'd had to use her imagination with Tanner. She'd imagined he was a good guy deep down. She had no need to exercise her imaginative skills when it came to Sean, because Sean was solid, true to the bone.

Her hands tingled as she placed them on the back of his neck and drew him closer, and she heard his quick intake of breath. How many years had she longed to do just this? How much time had she spent wishing that his brotherly hugs and teasing and friendship meant more? How often had she suspected that he might feel the same?

She pulled away with awful reluctance. "Sean, I'm sorry. This isn't right."

He caught her hand. "Why, Tess?"

She squeezed his strong hand, relished his touch, then pulled from it and shifted through the sand and water. "We just can't do this. We can't risk what we have with a mistake."

"You think being together is a mistake?"

"Earlier this year, I got a man killed because I was reluctant to break off a hopeless relationship."

"I'm not Tanner. And this isn't hopeless. In fact, I'd say there's a lot of hope."

"Oh, Sean," she whispered, reaching up to caress his jaw, "I know that. Even Megan pointed it out to me quite firmly today."

"Really?" He grinned and placed his hand over hers. "Well, she's a doctor, so she's pretty smart," he drawled in his teasing voice.

Again, Tess withdrew. His grin died. There was nothing she wanted more than to stay right here, let him take her in his arms again. Maybe she would even initiate the next kiss....

"The fact stands that I'm not risking more. Not now. Especially not you, of all people."

"And by that, you mean because I'm too weak and helpless to protect myself."

"By that, I mean because you're too precious for me to bear losing."

For a moment, he didn't reply, just gazed into her eyes and held her hostage. "Those are heady words," he said at last.

"Don't you think it's a little late to disengage our friendship in case someone's watching?"

"No. Keeping my distance is safer for everyone." She handed him the rest of her bread. "I need to take a walk and clear my head, okay?"

He sighed. "I could walk with you, make sure you're safe."

She couldn't help smiling. "Then my head wouldn't clear."

"So, you're saying I clog your sinuses?"

"No, just my gray matter." She turned and splashed back to the sun-warmed sand.

Sean walked from the water, watching Tess stroll away, head bowed, shoulders slumped. Though he was still stunned by the kiss, he felt chilled to the bone. He hadn't meant for that to happen. How could he have been so thoughtless? Maybe he hadn't learned as much these past months as he'd thought.

And yet, for just that moment, he and Tess had been simply two people who cared about each other. A lot. More than a lot. She'd been laughing, happy, playing with the birds. She'd carried her burden for so many months—longer, actually, than he'd carried his own.

As he continued to watch her, unable to look away, the right leg of her jeans unfolded to her ankle. She didn't stop and straighten it. She looked so forlorn.

Sean started after her. He didn't care if he messed up her brain matter. Their discussion wasn't over. No way was he taking that kiss back or apologizing for it. If that kiss had erased just a tiny portion of her sad focus, then he'd done the right thing.

He'd gone maybe ten yards when his cell phone buzzed. It was Gerard's ring tone, and Sean knew he wouldn't call unless it was necessary.

He flipped the phone open, watching Tess disappear around the curve of a sandy bank. "What's up?"

"Are you anywhere near a television?"

"On the beach."

"Great," Gerard muttered.

"Why?"

"I'm in our store, and Colleen has one of the secondhand televisions set up for the customers to check out. Just listen."

Sean heard the tinny sound of a voice. It got clearer. It was a newscaster talking about late-breaking news in Corpus Christi. "...serving tainted food to the homeless. One person has already died, and others are still ill, a significant majority Mexican. The name of the deceased is being withheld pending contact with next of kin."

Sean groaned. Gerard was understandably upset about this. But he didn't come back on the line. More news coming?

"A recent investigation has uncovered evidence that the hit-and-run accident that resulted in the death of Austin's country music talent Tanner Jackson in March may have been intentional. A person of interest is Jackson's former publicist, Tess Vance, who turned over her agency to associates and disappeared from the scene in Austin soon after her client's death. It was noted that this same Tess Vance is connected to the Vance Rescue Mission, though she has seldom been known to fraternize with the Hispanic population of homeless who frequent the mission..."

When Gerard's voice came back on the line, it was cold, hard, filled with anger. "No suspicion at all lingered on Tess. She was cleared that first night, and now they're trying to make her out to be a bigot. If I had my hands on that talking head right now I'd—"

"You'd stop yourself before you mangled his body," Sean said softly, though his voice held the edge of his own anger. "Anybody could have reported the poisoning, but nobody knows yet what made our people sick. That report was nothing but supposition and fiction. Which channel?"

"Our own Corpus Christi Eleven. I'll call our attorneys."

"The TV station's treading a fine line, as always, but technically, I don't think there's anything we can do to them."

"I'm calling, anyway. Do you realize how much damage they've done to us today?"

"Immeasurable."

"If this spreads, donations will dry up, both in finances and dry goods for the store. We wouldn't be able to feed and house nearly as many on our own."

"Gerard, don't get carried away. One television station released a few seconds of scandal in the middle of the day."

"It'll hit the six o'clock news; others will pick it up. Too juicy to resist."

"My station's not picking it up."

Gerard was silent for a moment, then, "Who made the connection with Tess? I think her instincts are right on the mark. I think she's still being stalked, Sean."

The thought had been on Sean's mind, too.

"Is she there with you?" Gerard asked.

"Not far away."

"Could you have been followed?"

"Not unless someone's using hi-tech equipment. I watched."

"Did you see anyone unusual at the mission this morning after Stud died? Has Tess mentioned anything strange?"

"Only the influx of sick people." Sean started walking down the beach after Tess. "Wait. Yes." He stopped, recalling the details of what he'd seen. "There was a woman there when Stud died. She was just one of the onlookers, didn't have a camera or recorder that I saw, but she was carrying a satchel over her shoulder, was nicely dressed and didn't appear to belong. I didn't see her leave until you were talking on the phone to Megan later."

"A woman with a satchel? That's not much to go on, Sean."

"Medium blond hair, long, parted in the middle and tied back. About five foot seven, black dress, heels, beige coat. Moved quickly, as if she had somewhere to go. That's why she didn't fit in. I didn't recognize her this morning; last time I met her, she had hair that was short, red and curly."

"You met her?"

"Name's on the tip of my tongue. Something sweet… Taffy…no—anyway, she applied for a position at the station. My assistant, Cathy, was impressed by her resume, but when she followed up on it, she didn't receive enough acceptable references. The woman was a freelance reporter who wrote a lot for the gossip rags. A lot of unsubstantiated information on the resume."

"Then why would a television station take her word as fact?" Gerard asked.

"Rush to get the news out first. Isn't that what Eleven always does?"

"You think it'll be in the papers tomorrow?"

"I'll do what I can to stop it. I know most of the media people in the area."

"How do you stop a domino from pushing the whole construction over?"

"Push back the other way."

"How could she have found out about Tess?"

"She could have been eavesdropping on Tess and me this morning in the clinic."

"Got a name yet?"

Sean remembered it, and his footsteps lengthened to catch up with Tess. "Sugar McCrae."

"Sounds like a nightclub dancer."

"I don't think it's her real name, but I'll check with Cathy. If that's what happened, then we may be able to breathe easier about a stalker."

"Let's not start breathing just yet. Our priority is Tess, but after that we have a whole building and street full of people to protect. You'd better warn Tess she'll probably receive a visit from a couple of homicide detectives. With even a slimy lead like that piece of filth from the TV station, they may check her out because she was suggested as a suspect."

"Maybe not, if they can call the team that worked on Jackson's case in Austin. Why don't you call the captain and give him a heads-up?"

"Good idea."

"I was just getting ready to call you. I received the results from the lab where I took the dirt that was tracked into Admin last night. This could mean nothing except that the intruder was from a ranch, but they found arsenic."

Gerard whistled. "Barnyards and old barns are likely to have some arsenic in them from fertilizer, though I don't think many of my ranching buddies use that anymore."

"You might have Megan call the lab, just in case, and have them narrow their search."

"I'll have her get on the phone now."

"And I'll get Tess and return to the mission. See you then." He closed the phone and went to find Tess. What had he been thinking when he allowed her to walk away alone? The stalker wasn't playing around, and no one could drop guard on Tess.

He broke into a jog and called her name.

SIX

Sean hadn't expected Tess to get so far in such a short period of time, and he hadn't realized how frantic he was to simply see her and assure himself she was safe. Gerard's overprotective, brotherly love was contagious.

Except Sean's love was not brotherly. Sure, he could feel brotherly about her when the occasion called for it, but he'd known for some time that his feelings for that beautiful, black-haired woman weren't comparable to Gerard's.

He called to her and saw her turn. For a moment, he couldn't bring himself to move farther. Looking at her wavy, long hair glowing in the sun, like the midnight sky scattered with stars, at her dark, inquisitive eyes, the gentle curve of her half smile, he wasn't sure he'd be able to say the words that would punch her to her knees.

"Sean?" She turned and walked back toward him. "What's wrong?"

Breathe. "I got a call from Gerard."

"What happened?"

The sound of foreboding in her voice squeezed his heart. With inopportune clarity, it hit home that the fond feelings, the attraction, the longing he felt for her were only symptoms of a much fiercer love. His compassion and potent need to protect her at all cost could consume him and keep him from telling her what she needed to know. For her own good, hard as it would be, he must warn her immediately about what they would find back at the clinic.

"Honey, I have to explain a few things to you, but you must remember that Gerard and I will be here for you at any time."

She stepped through the sand to him. "Trying to scare me?"

"I'm a little unnerved, myself. So is Gerard. Someone must have been eavesdropping on our conversation this morning in the clinic. That someone was a quasi reporter."

Her gaze clung to his as her eyes widened. "What could anyone have heard?"

He placed an arm around her shoulders and turned to walk with her back to the truck. As they walked, he explained about the earlier call, his suspicions about Sugar McCrae, and his conversation with Gerard in detail.

Tess was numb and shivering by the time they reached the truck. "What's wrong with this world?"

"A lot."

"How can professionals allow some sick woman to use smear tactics like this?"

"You're surprised? This is the channel you complained about because they took Carlotta's death so lightly two weeks ago."

"Which makes me wonder why they're suddenly so concerned about the homeless this week."

"Ratings."

"What if this…this Sugar McCrae was the one who hit Tanner?"

"Then we'll catch her, but we don't know for sure it was Sugar who shared the information. We can't jump to conclusions."

"What kind of a name is Sugar?"

"You sound just like your brother."

"I love my brother. But don't tell him I said that."

Sean chuckled. "Sugar is probably a nickname that became

her real name, kind of like Tess. I love the name Tess, by the way."

She allowed him to distract her with his deep, soothing voice. "I can't believe this is happening." No way could she hold the tears back or keep her teeth from chattering.

Sean put his arms around her and held her close for a long moment. She closed her eyes at the warmth of his body—and the true warmth of his strength and goodness and kind heart in what seemed to be a cold and bitter world right now. When had Sean developed the ability to make her feel as if everything would be okay? At least, most of the time.

"If we find out for sure this McCrae woman gave the report," she said, "I'm going to that television station, and I'm going to hunt her down and slap her silly."

Sean released her and opened the door. "You've never slapped anyone in your life."

"You're right. I'll mace her instead."

Sean grinned down at her. "At least, you're getting your weird sense of humor back. What we're going to do right now is get you into the truck and get the heater on, and we're going back to the mission." He reached over the seat and pulled out an extra jacket, wrapped it around her shoulders and pulled it tight. "Step in."

She did as she was told. She felt as if she'd been kicked in the gut, but worse, the people who would suffer the most over this were those who could least afford to lose more—they didn't have a place to lay their heads, didn't have jobs or bank accounts to fall back on.

"I know some of the folks at Channel Eleven," Sean said as he got in and started the engine.

"Do you know where the general manager lives?"

"I have his phone number, and I can talk to him. At this point, we won't do more than that."

"You think it'll do any good?"

"Never can tell."

"You know what needs to happen, don't you?" Tess pulled

the jacket more tightly around her shoulders. Even the heat coming from the vents didn't warm her.

"You want to mace him, too?"

"It's a thought."

"All forms of media need to be gagged?"

"It wouldn't hurt."

"Then my station would also be gagged. A lot more people would be out of work."

"Then maybe Sugar McCrae would be out of work and beholden to a mission to feed her. But that's not what I meant. Sean, I need to leave. Stay away from the mission completely."

"That's probably a good idea."

She glanced at him.

He gave her a half smile. "Surprised you, didn't I? Love to do that, you know."

"You agree with me." Somehow, that frightened her more than anything else that had happened today. "And Gerard?"

"Haven't talked to him about it, but he probably wants you out of the building, too."

She couldn't panic. Tess took a slow, deep breath and let it out more slowly yet. Deep breathing. Now was not the time to lose her nerve. She had to think straight. Or she could just allow Sean to drive, and she could shut up for a few minutes. Watch the water as she sat back and tried to get warm. Relish Sean's closeness. He was beside her. He'd kissed her. He cared for her.

He could be in danger because of her.

She sat up straighter. "The zinger is that someone leaked that the attack on Tanner wasn't an accident."

"I know. It's possible this woman found a bad cop, who talked after she recognized the Vance name and traced it to your agency in Austin. Thanks to your hard work, Tanner was seeing some fame before he died, at least in Texas. Even for a pseudo reporter, it wouldn't have been hard to put two and two together."

"But she didn't come up with four, she came up with eight.

Gerard is convinced enough to order a toxicology panel. And you and Gerard both agree I need to leave."

"The mission. The building, Tess. Not home."

"You think there's danger. Gerard thinks there is."

Sean turned a corner and pressed on the accelerator, checked the rearview mirror, adjusted it, and settled into his seat. "We're still cops at heart, so you know we're going to be cautious with the life of the woman we both love."

There was silence in the truck except for the quiet engine and the thud of Tess's heart in her ears, her uneven breathing, the powerful echo of Sean's words.

Everything fell into place. Of all the horrific times for her to suddenly realize the truth about her own heart, to perceive what an impact Sean had made on her since their first meeting all those years ago. To recognize the first, tender shoots of love as it had grown for him, gotten stronger.

And she hadn't given it an opportunity to grow. Instead, she'd rejected the reality of Sean's place in her life to pursue a dream that had fallen to dust at the death of a man she should never have told "I love you."

"We have a lot in common, you and I," Sean said above the rumble of the engine.

She glanced at him again and saw the way his strong jaw muscles flexed. How familiar that silhouette was to her. And how exceptional.

"We both feel guilt about the death of a loved one. Now me, I'm guilty because I helped create that little life in the first place. I knew there could be consequences to my actions, but I tuned them out."

"You asked her to marry you."

"Yep, I know."

"You did all you knew to do. You begged Kari Ann until the last minute not to have that abortion."

"Yes, but you see, my decision should have been made sooner." He glanced at Tess. "You were a victim. Still are. I was a culprit. Big difference."

She felt fresh tears burn her eyes at the gentleness of his voice, the glance he sent her that showed his heart so clearly. How could she have missed that look before? It had been there, reflected on his face so many times when he looked at her.

"You became a victim, too," Tess said. "And I hated seeing you go through that. You're such a good, good man, Sean. You always have been. I know this may sound corny, but I've always thought you had such a deep, beautiful spirit about you. When I'm with you, I'm safe."

"Aw, that's just because I'm a cop with a gun."

"No gun could have stopped Stud from being killed."

Sean studied the road for a moment, his dark blue-green gaze intent on the cars passing them. "In a way, you might say Stud kind of killed himself. Oh, I know he didn't make himself sick this morning, but no one else died. The others were feeling better last I checked. Stud had already destroyed his ability to rebound from that kind of hit."

"I need to leave Corpus Christi."

"No, you don't."

"It seems wherever I go, trouble has begun to follow."

"Don't get ahead of yourself."

"I'm endangering Gerard by living with him. It's best if I just disappear."

"You do, I'm going with you."

"I'm serious, Sean."

He paused for a moment, looked at her, then back at the road. "So am I. You have loved ones who can be hurt, whether you're with them or not. If you leave, I will be more than hurt. I will be devastated. That may make me sound weak and vulnerable, but I don't care."

Her eyes smarted with moisture. "Oh, Sean." She felt the same. Could this man truly be anointed by God as her perfect match here on earth? "But if Stud's death is a result of intentional poisoning because of me, then that means whoever commits the deed does it when I can see the destruction and be wounded by it. And there are a lot of people at risk this time."

"Big if, Tess. We're talking about a possibility, not a probability at this point."

"Too much of a possibility."

"You're not going away by yourself. Gerard's got a big house, and we can move the whole admin operation to the ranch until this mess is settled. You're not going out on your own."

Those words made Tess feel strangely comforted. She gazed out at the gunmetal-gray water reflecting clouds that had moved in when she wasn't paying attention. No more blue skies today. How appropriate.

Sean reached across and tapped her on the arm. "I think that's the first time in your life that someone has told you what you may or may not do, and you didn't blow a fuse."

"You told me to get in the truck, and I did that."

"Sure, but this here's your only mode of transportation back to the mission. You're not much good at taking orders."

She had to agree. He was right. Of course, if she wanted to take off on her own, she could do it without asking anyone's permission, and if Gerard had said the same thing, she'd have argued.

"You're never too bossy around me."

"I value my life."

She grinned. "You're just not the bossy type."

"You've never come to the radio station, have you?"

"I've been in quite a few radio stations, newspaper offices, television studios, but I've never been to your place. Maybe I should."

"Later, when this is all over, you can come and see how bossy I really am."

She nodded and stared back out the window again. "When this is all over. You sound so sure of it."

"I have no doubt. We're under attack right now, and that's not going to be a way of life from now on. Have some faith in your brother and me. Have some faith in God. It's a test. You can't just close up shop on your life because the devil's taking a poke at you. You've got more faith than that, Tess. I know that for a fact."

His words covered her, flowed through her, destroyed those little pinpricks of fear that had caused such agony for so long. Something about being with Sean had always made her feel a little higher, a little sharper than usual and at the same time, more peaceful.

When he'd guarded her in Austin, they'd talked for hours in the evenings after she finished for the day. She'd shared stories of her childhood and her job, but had never confided in him about her intention to break her engagement with Tanner until this morning.

Sean had told her about growing up in San Antonio, about losing his mother when he was thirteen, about his father's struggle to raise three kids on a paramedic's salary and unreal hours.

"Sean?"

"Yeah."

"Are you going to wreck this truck if I tell you I might love you, too?" Was she crazy to say those words? No. She did have faith. Sean's words had only reawakened it for her.

Sean pulled in behind the mission building where the employees and volunteers parked their cars. He stopped beside Tess's blue Cooper and walked around to open her door. He'd had to fight her tooth and nail over this opening-the-door thing, and he'd won. For once. So, maybe he was bossier than she'd admitted.

He felt as if maybe his face was glowing or something. Had to be. Impossible to get those four words out of his mind: *I might love you...*

She slid from the seat, and just stood there for a moment. She just stood there, looking up at him.

He realized soon enough that he was blocking her from doing anything else, so he stepped aside. Still, she gazed up at him without moving, dark eyes filled with silent thoughts.

How he wished she'd share them all with him. She once again reached up and placed her hand on his jawline.

"Thank you, Sean." Her voice was husky.

"Welcome, ma'am."

"What now?"

"You go home. I'll call the ranch and tell the hands you're coming and make sure they watch out for you. I'll send Mamie or Joni out with your files to get everything set up out there. Keep the dogs with you, keep your mace nearby but practice how to aim that stuff, because if you miss and get yourself at the wrong time, you're in deep trouble."

"Where are you going?"

"I'm going to touch base with Gerard, then go to the radio station to make some calls and do some damage control if I can."

She released a breath. "Good."

He narrowed his eyes at her. "Just like that? You trust me?"

"I do."

"So you're not going to question how I'm going to do it or make any suggestions?"

"You're getting me confused with Gerard, Sean. Shame on you. He's the bossy one."

"Okay, but you understand that the silence has been broken about Tanner's death?"

"Not really."

That's what he was afraid of. If this whole thing worked out as he feared it would—worst case scenario—Tess was going to be ready to mace him. But he didn't know what would happen yet.

"I'll make it work, Tess."

"Make that station look ridiculous. Drop their ratings," she said. "Put them out of business."

"I'll just have to play it by ear, Tess. I'll do whatever it takes to protect you and the mission, but it may become public."

"You're a hero, Sean. You always have been." She clicked

the unlock remote in her hand. It was as if she hadn't heard his words.

He grinned down at her. He wanted to take her far from here and help her forget how much she'd endured, but sometimes folks just had to face things and get through them. This was one of those times. He pressed a kiss on her forehead, opened her door and held it for her to get in. "Call me immediately if you have a problem."

"I will."

He closed the door and watched her drive away. How he wished this past year had never happened, that she'd never become engaged to the wrong man, that he'd never invited Kari Ann to dinner.

He was beginning to wonder, however, if the stalker might still have stalked Tess even without her connection to Tanner. He and Gerard had done extensive background research on all of Tess's former employees, on a long list of Tanner's acquaintances, practically on anyone who'd looked cross-eyed at Tess in the past five years. Nothing looked suspicious except for the embezzler, and he was behind bars, with no bitter family members or friends to be found. Apparently, the thief wasn't a real charming guy.

Sean couldn't help wondering if they'd missed something. Or someone.

SEVEN

When Sean entered the mission proper he found Gerard waiting at the back door. His hair stood out in strange directions and his eyes looked shadowed. "Where's Tess going?"

Sean glanced around them. No one was nearby listening, but who knew? "Into hiding."

Gerard caught his look. "Let's take a walk."

"I need to get to the station to try to stop this thing."

"Short jog, then."

They crossed the parking lot to the sidewalk and strolled south at a good clip.

"I'm going to have Mamie Park take all of Tess's files, computer, everything to the ranch, where we can set up a room for her to work," Sean said.

"Nope."

"Why not? Tess wants to keep helping—"

"Not Mamie. Not Joni. I'll take everything myself."

Sean stopped. Gerard kept going a few more feet before stopping. When he turned back, there was a look of deep regret on his face. "The Park sisters are on my suspect list, Sean. I did a more thorough background check on them. Joni's name was never on the title to anything, and we just figured that, with Mamie being the older sister, Mamie took the largest portion of responsibility. Now, it seems she was the only one on the title because Joni had just moved in with her, only a few weeks before the building burned down."

"You don't think Joni's guilty of anything?"

"I'm just being cautious. Some records suggest Joni was in Austin before she moved in with her sister."

"How much did they suggest it?"

"Not enough to prove anything, only some phone calls to Mamie from an Austin area code, but that's enough for me."

"Joni seems to like to kick up her heels a bit, and she's awfully young. With their parents dead, Mamie probably didn't have a lot of control over her willful little sister."

"All true, but Joni's impulsive, and the girl has a temper. That's all I'm saying about it for now."

"Okay, what else have you got?"

"I checked out this Sugar McCrae. Birth name was Sherleen. She had mixed references from former employers."

"Let me guess," Sean said. "Her bad references come from employers who found out she didn't always substantiate her stories."

"Good guess. I also called our attorneys, and it would take a lot of money, even with some pro bono, to slap a malicious slander charge on Channel Eleven—and it would probably be impossible to win."

"So we don't have a case."

"I don't want to pour a lot of money down that hole if we're going to lose anyway, and if we can't make headway against the rumors, we're going to need all the money we can save to keep the mission going."

"Then I need to get to my own office at my own station and start putting out some fires." Sean turned back toward the parking lot.

Gerard followed him. "How's Tess doing?"

"You know your sister, she's a fighter."

"You sure she's not driving to the TV station now to kick some teeth in?"

"Now, Gerard, when was your sweet little sister ever violent?"

"So she's doing okay?"

"She'll get through this. We all will."

"So…you two took a romantic little drive, huh?"

"I took your sister away from the mission for a break."

"Uh-huh. And did you two share makeup tips or something?"

Sean scowled at his friend.

Gerard chuckled. "You might want to dab some of that color off your mouth before you walk into your station. You know, let them know you're still a manly man."

Sean took a swipe at his mouth with the back of his hand while Gerard walked through the back door of the mission, laughing. It was a pretty color, but it looked better on the woman Sean had kissed.

Tess slumped into Gerard's kitchen from the garage after being stopped twice by ranch hands on the long driveway to the house. They wanted to know if she was okay. True to his word, Sean had called to alert her protectors.

She felt as if she was being wrapped in a warm, down comforter by Sean and Gerard. She'd be surprised if Hans didn't call her within the hour to check on her.

She heard the rumble of eight eager feet as Roxie and Romper raced each other to see who could jump up and lick her face first. As it happened, they both met her at the same time and nearly knocked her over.

"Yuck, Romper. What have you been eating?" She couldn't help laughing as the larger male Doberman smiled up at her with devotion and adoration until Roxie knocked him aside and whined her welcome. Against her better judgment, Tess dropped to her knees and allowed the animals to smother her in their own brand of slobbering, whining, all-inclusive love.

She was interrupted a few moments later by the jingle of her cell phone. Why had she allowed Megan to set Sean's ring tone to Christmas music? The doctor had an interesting sense of irony.

"Home yet?" Sean asked after she answered.

"Yep, covered in dog spit."

"That's the best medicine. Why didn't you tell me I had your lip stuff on my face?"

Tess caught her breath, and then she burst into giggles. "Oh, Sean, I'm so sorry. I didn't…honestly, I wasn't, um, paying attention to…I was distracted."

"Yeah, me too, but that's okay, because your brother caught me in time to stop me from embarrassing myself."

She groaned. "He's going to milk this for all it's worth."

"Just because he's jealous. I don't think he'd mind if our Dr. Bradley wore bright purple lipstick and kissed him all over his face."

Tess sank onto the center of the living room sofa so Romper and Roxie could each claim a side. "I'm going to have to watch that next time."

"That's exactly what I wanted you to say."

She smiled.

"There's going to be a next time, then?" Sean asked.

Oh, she hoped so. But she couldn't bring herself to say it. Not yet. Not with so many questions and so much danger hovering.

"Tess, why don't you call Megan to spend the night? Gerard's probably going to spend as much time as possible at the mission. I'll be going back there as soon as I tidy up at the station and do my damage control, then return to spell Gerard."

"Sounds good. Tomorrow's Megan's day off. Dr. Bowling is volunteering the day."

"If word gets out, he'll be swamped. Everybody loves him."

"Because he treats every patient like a human being. Like Megan does."

"Yeah, like you do. Like Gerard does." Sean chuckled. "I'm not sorry Gerard discovered makeup on my face."

She sighed. "Thank you."

"And you know what else?"

"What?" she asked, sinking more deeply into the soft cushion, feeling warm all over.

"I'm not sorry that I love you."

She closed her eyes and laid her head back. "Neither am I."

Three hours after his last talk with Tess, Sean slammed down his phone and leaned back in his office chair. No promises from anyone. It seemed every member of every form of media in the area was trying to dig more deeply into the Tanner Jackson death, and though he'd been assured that their reports would be grounded in fact and not hearsay, he'd also been harassed by three people to give them Tess's cell phone number so they could talk to the source. He gave them something, all right, but it wasn't Tess's phone number. They were not amused.

He glanced at the clock and braced himself. If someone really did have a smear campaign planned for Tess, he was going to stop it in its tracks, but it was going to be ugly for everyone, especially the one person he most wanted to protect. He had to call her and talk to her about what he was about to tell the public.

Before he could touch the phone, it rang. He picked up to hear Gerard saying, "Bingo."

"What?"

"Arsenic was found in the blood tests. Now we know how the poison was delivered."

"How's that?"

"Colleen came to help out in the kitchen today because we're vetting our help so closely, and she just happens to love hot sauce on everything she eats. She caught the scent of garlic in one of the Tabasco sauce bottles, and she called my attention to it. I took it for testing, and we have our answer."

"Someone put arsenic in the hot sauce?"

"That's right."

"Anyone could have done that."

"Yep. It's the only thing we keep in bottles and not individual packets. Anyone off the street could have done it."

"Tess and I had a hot sauce competition last night, but we

used the habaneras sauce Sandra Mancillas makes. Angel gave it to us himself."

"No wonder you two didn't get sick. They keep the good stuff for their favorite people."

"What now?"

"Police. I'm calling the captain now."

"May I report it on the air?"

"Do whatever you have to, just keep our suspect's name out of it."

"You trust me, then, huh?"

"With my life. Even with my sister."

The clock was ticking. "Okay, then, I'm going to have to do this on the fly. It's time for me to kick Joe from his microphone."

Joe, of course, was confused when Sean whispered the change of plans next to his left shoulder.

"What, boss?"

"I'm doing the first portion of the evening news."

"Since when?"

"Since three minutes ago. Out of the chair." He tipped the big guy to the side, and Joe got up, scratching his head and frowning.

Sean took the DJ's head mic, sat down and waited for his signal, ignoring the puzzled looks he received from other members of his staff, regretting the fact that he didn't have time to call Tess and explain what he was doing and why.

The signal came.

"Good evening. This is Sean Torrance, owner of KSFJ radio station, with late-breaking news from the Vance Rescue Mission. An earlier broadcast from a Corpus Christi television station reported an outbreak of food poisoning at the rescue mission's soup kitchen. The source of contamination has since been isolated and confirmed as arsenic by a local lab. The police are being notified and all workers and volunteers are being required to take a course in security protocol." He only hoped his buddies on the police force would forgive him for getting the jump on them this one time.

"KSFJ advises other soup kitchens, shelters and missions in the region to increase security and closely vet all employees and volunteers with comprehensive background checks. It is our goal to protect and serve those in our society who are most vulnerable.

"The co-owner and founder of the Vance Rescue Mission, Gerard Vance, has assured me that security measures have already been taken to protect the people who depend on his mission for food and shelter. It is felt that the contamination was deliberate, and the method used to spread the poison has been removed."

He swallowed and decided on some aggressive words.

"Due to incomplete substantiation, it was also reported earlier today by a Corpus Christi television station that a Vance family member, Tess Vance, was a person of interest in the poisoning at the mission, as well as in the death of her client, Tanner Jackson, a musician in Austin, Texas, earlier in the year. This station has an eye-witness account—"

He paused, both for effect and for courage.

"—that not only was Miss Vance cleared of any suspicion by Austin police immediately after Jackson's death, but she served as a witness to the fact that the hit-and-run incident was, in fact, intentional, as he was crossing the street at the time of the incident to visit with Miss Vance, who was his fiancé."

As soon as the words were out of his mouth, he couldn't help questioning himself, even as he continued with the report, including information about the threatening notes. There would be no dead air on KSFJ.

"Please stay tuned for more news as we receive it."

Before he was finished, he signaled Joe to trade places with him, and the program continued without interruption.

He walked out of the station through the back door, calling over his shoulder that he wasn't accepting calls. There would be a lot of them. He'd made a brazen move, and there would be waves from every direction. How could he explain that he had no choice? He had to turn the tables on Channel Eleven before they could continue to slice Tess's character to pieces.

He'd had to reveal the engagement, the threatening notes. And he'd had to make that revelation with force to show that he had information no other media in the area possessed. He could only pray that the difference between the truth and rumor would be obvious to honest listeners.

Now it would be necessary to decide what to announce on the air tomorrow, and possibly for days to come, in order to keep the story moving in the right direction.

He would not say anything about the possibility that someone might have killed Tanner because of the engagement, but if Channel Eleven wanted a battle over the airwaves, they would get one, and on this one subject, he would win.

He flipped open his cell phone, pressed speed dial and stared up at the dark, starless sky.

Megan answered Tess's cell. "Are you trying to get yourself maimed?"

"She heard, huh?"

"Both of us heard. You know Tess never listens to the radio, don't you?"

"Yeah."

"But tonight, she just had to see if anyone else was going to try to ambush the mission or rip her to shreds."

"Ouch."

"You can bet she was surprised."

"She does realize why I gave that report, doesn't she?"

"I don't know what she realizes. I'm not sure she does. Give her some time."

"Where is she?"

"I think she's out in the barn with Romper and Roxie, preparing to commit suicide by horse."

"She's riding Scorpio?" Gerard's palomino stallion was not good under a saddle.

"She's considering it, but I'm counting on her common sense to make her rethink her options. It would be a painful death. I offered to let her use my pistol as an alternative."

"I'm coming out there."

"Doesn't Gerard need you at the mission?"

"I'll call him. He could probably use help, but there are enough vetted employees and volunteers willing to work extra shifts because of this mess. I think he can do without me long enough for me to reassure Tess. Have the police arrived?"

"They were here about forty-five minutes ago, talked to Tess about where she was yesterday, told her they already had the police report from Austin, and they just sat and jabbered awhile. You know how Benjamin Delmonico seems to have a thing for her."

Delmonico had better back off. "So it was casual and friendly."

"That's right. One hurdle cleared. Head on out to the barn when you get here. She'll need her animal therapy session, even if she doesn't ride."

"I'll be there in about twenty minutes."

"Maybe that'll give her time to get some of the angst out of her system before you offer yourself for target practice."

After he disconnected, he called Gerard and explained his plan, promising to return to the mission so Gerard could go home and get some sleep.

It would be okay. As soon as he faced Tess.

EIGHT

Tess stopped at Scorpio's stall and petted his soft nose. The gorgeous, golden stallion was a pussy cat when one wasn't actually on his back trying to tell him which way to go. Tess felt so filled with furious energy right now that she'd probably be able to handle him tonight, but the last time she'd tried to ride him, she'd ended up face-first in the muddy pasture.

She reached for his bridle, then started to open his stall. For some reason, Romper and Roxie whined. She glanced at them to see if they might have heard something or someone approaching. Two pairs of dark, anxious eyes were directed at her.

She sighed. "You know, I can ride a horse, kids."

Romper walked to the stall door and parked himself in front of it on his haunches.

"Oh, for goodness' sake, Romper, I know how to take care of myself."

Roxie whined and crawled on her belly to Tess's feet. She rested her chin across Tess's right boot.

"Since when do you dogs have such long memories?" Okay, Scorpio had thrown her more than once, and since the dogs went wherever she went on the ranch, they'd witnessed those ignominious incidents. Still, she couldn't allow Gerard's two Dobermans, who, come to think of it, took after their owner in many ways, to tell her what to do. Her life had been turned upside down enough today. She needed to regain some control.

She pulled the stall door open to the sound of Romper's irritable growl. Yep, just like his owner. Scorpio nuzzled her face and actually leaned into her as she stepped up to his huge, warm column of neck and wrapped her arms around it, leaning against his solid body. She breathed in the air of the barn and allowed the scents of hay, grain, dust and horse hide to comfort her. She pushed this frightening, wonderful, horrible, painful day aside and allowed the memories of her childhood to fill her mind, when all was right in her world, and her biggest challenge was figuring out how to break the rules—meaning, ride her mare before her chores were finished.

A soft thud drew her attention to the half wall of the stall, where Hobbit, the fluffy, fat tabby barn cat landed with a leap from the upper rafters. The cat had a purr that could reverberate throughout the barn. Tess reached up and allowed Hobbit to nuzzle her fingers.

"You look sleepy, Hobbit. Did I interrupt your rest?"

The cat trilled, reaching out a paw in her customary bid for attention.

Gerard had nailed some boards diagonally from the side of the wall to the front, where he could sit and visit with his horse. Tess sank onto them, and immediately Hobbit climbed down to her lap while the dogs entered the stall and settled at her feet, apparently relieved she wasn't saddling Scorpio. The horse nuzzled the cat and then Tess's face, his forelock tickling her skin. His breath smelled as sweet as the hay he'd been eating.

With a sigh, Tess leaned back.

After growing up on a cattle ranch, she knew animals. She'd learned long ago that her mare, Josie, could pick up on her moods. So could two of the three mutts she and her brothers had rescued from the shelter and the two stray cats they'd given a home. When she had her heart broken by some boy in school—it had happened a few times—she'd go home and sulk on the front porch, and the dogs would surround her, one of them because he wanted his ears scratched, the other two for commiseration.

Or she could lie down on the living room floor, and her cats would lie on top of her or curl up against her side and purr until she felt better. And she always felt better after her therapy sessions.

Gerard accused her of having some secret animal charm, but Scorpio had proven otherwise. Of course, maybe she couldn't transmit her closeness through a cold, hard saddle. Next time, she'd ride him bareback. But she decided, reluctantly, that wouldn't be tonight. Romper might try harder to convince her to see reason, and she didn't want the seat of her jeans ripped out by Doberman teeth.

Romper and Roxie weren't mere pets. They had been taught not to trust strangers, and in order for anyone to get into the house, that person first had to be introduced to both dogs by someone they trusted. For some reason, since last March when Tess moved in, they had become much more possessive of her…almost as if they knew…

By the time she heard the sound of an approaching engine, she was feeling better, and Romper had wandered away, assured somehow that she had decided not to ride tonight.

It wasn't until the engine died that she realized it wasn't Gerard's. He would have pulled into the garage.

So much for the therapy session. She gave an irritable sigh when she recognized the sound of Sean's footsteps coming toward the barn. Scorpio snorted.

"Tess, you're not planning to ride that spoiled brat tonight, are you?" Sean called from the barn door.

She gave Hobbit a final hug and lifted her onto the top of the wall. "Not the wisest greeting for you right now, Torrance." She stepped forward and wrapped her arms once more around Scorpio's neck, trying to soak up his strength, and then she picked up the bridle and waited for Roxie to precede her from the stall. Scorpio tried to follow, but she pressed his nose back and shut him in.

Sean was standing with his hand out when she turned around. He took the bridle from her and hung it on its peg, then turned back to her. "We need to talk."

"I can't talk right now. I feel as if I've been kicked in the stomach."

"You said you trusted me."

"That was before you betrayed me."

"What part of 'going public' did you not understand?"

"The part that nobody mentioned on television today. The part about my engagement to Tanner, which will, most likely, make me Public Enemy Number One."

"You were cleared by the police, remember?"

"But the police never found the killer, and in the eyes of the people who don't know any better, if they can't find the killer, they might well be overlooking the most obvious suspect. Aside from all that, you announced, over the most popular radio station within listening distance, information you were privileged to know only as a trusted friend."

"There's that word again. Can't you continue to trust me? Don't you know me by now? Will you at least give me a chance to explain why I did what I did?"

"Couldn't you have done that before you gave the report? Thirty seconds to at least warn me?"

"Tess, I spent the whole afternoon, from the time I left the mission until two minutes before the news hour, calling the newspapers, television and radio stations in an effort to stop this bomb from exploding on us. They didn't want to listen."

"Because Eleven is making a bid for top ratings and the others are scrambling to keep up."

"That's right, and Eleven's doing it unethically."

"So with your unique efforts to stop it from happening," she said, turning away to pet Scorpio's ears, which were perked forward, "you probably solidified your position at the top."

There was silence. Tess nearly cringed at her own words. She knew Sean better than this. She'd known him a long time, long enough to know he had no hidden agenda.

And yet, she still felt so betrayed. She turned back to find him watching her, the dark aqua of his eyes nearly black.

"I'd have preferred a macing," he said quietly.

She closed her eyes. "I'm sorry. That was out of line."

"As I told you, the story was already out, and I had to lead it back in the right direction so it would be the truth instead of a smear campaign against you and the mission, and in order to do that, I had to introduce fresh information, not recycled bits and pieces. I had to convince the listeners that I knew what I was talking about. I could only do that with fresh material no one else could have had. It needed to be surprising."

"Oh, it was."

"A lot of people depend on that mission, and if we lost support because the local news stations and papers convinced the public not to donate items for resale, not to shop in our store, not to give to feed and house the hungry—"

"I know, Sean, okay?" she snapped. "You don't have to preach to me."

"Really? Because it sounds to me as if you think I'm the bad guy in all this."

"What's your morning news going to be?" she asked.

"I haven't decided yet."

She still stung from his news report, and she couldn't help it. His anger at her reaction just made it sting worse. "Why don't you tell them I've left Corpus Christi?"

"Because you're not leaving."

She turned and glared at him. "You don't have the right to tell me what I can and cannot do, where I can and cannot go. You may spread my secrets all over town, but you can't tell anyone what I'm doing next, because believe me, you don't know."

She left him standing in the barn and returned to the house, Romper and Roxie walking beside her. Tears finally spread across her face as if there'd been a cloudburst.

Sean forced himself not to slam the door of his truck. He'd learned long ago how to handle his anger the proper way, and making loud noises and breaking things was not proper. Besides, he didn't want Tess to be any more convinced that he was actually angry with her. He wasn't. He had, in fact, betrayed her. There'd been no way around it, and he'd do the same thing again if he had it to do over, but her private life had been offered up as a sacrifice on the altar of public gossip. He hadn't drawn first blood, but he had to continue the fight.

Tess must feel as if the knife had been buried to the hilt in her back. He'd hoped she would be more understanding, but then, what if the situation had been reversed? What if she'd gone to the airwaves with his dirty secret? How would he feel if he heard her announcing to all of Corpus Christi that he'd gotten a woman pregnant, that that woman had aborted his baby?

Would he trust her after that? Probably not.

He thought about what she'd told him, that he should announce she had left Corpus Christi. Even in the midst of a meltdown, she'd shown finesse. That was exactly what he needed to do. There was an upside to that and a downside. Upside was, whoever had poisoned their people would probably leave them alone. Downside was, whoever had poisoned their people would probably disappear, making it more difficult for the police—or Gerard and Sean—to catch their culprit. That meant Tess would continue to be stalked.

He glanced at the house, where light leaked past the closed blinds. Why couldn't he have been more sympathetic? More apologetic? Why had he fought with her when what she'd needed was a shoulder to cry on?

And he wanted it to be his shoulder. But Gerard had to be beat, and there was more work to do at the mission. Megan's shoulder would have to do.

Tess tumbled onto her back on the living room carpet and pillowed her head with her arms. "How could this happen?"

Megan sank into Gerard's recliner. "So, you and Sean aren't speaking now?"

"Oh, we're speaking all right."

"So, you're officially having your first fight, then."

Tess rolled to her side. "My life is a wreck, and you're making jokes."

"Oh, honey, I'm just pointing out the obvious. Sure, your first fight is painful right now, but it can solidify and deepen a relationship."

"Or kill it before it begins." The floor was getting hard, even with cushy carpet, so Tess transferred to the sofa before the dogs could find her lying there and get comfortable on top of her. "All the patients were better tonight?"

"Every one of them. They're still weak, but the worst of the poisoning has passed."

"From hot sauce."

"Angel and Sandra probably saved you and Sean—and probably many others—from a miserable day by bringing Sandra's own sauce from home."

"Megan, am I overreacting?"

"Nope."

"But you think Sean was right to do what he did?"

"Yep."

"You just don't intend to take sides on this thing, do you?"

"I'm on both sides. So is Gerard, just so you know. You and Sean are both strong people who care about others, and you're caught in a clash between good and evil. Literally. Sean's fighting it the only way he knows how, and I'm just glad he is who he is. If not for him, we might not have a good chance of winning this fight."

"He didn't warn me."

"Are you sure?"

"Well, okay, he didn't warn me about exactly what he was going to say."

"Sometimes it's easier to apologize than ask permission, but brace yourself, Tess, because if he knows more secrets about this whole thing that he hasn't shared—and I know there's at least one more secret—then he may feel pressured to tell those, too."

"He'll spill about my intention to break the engagement the night Tanner died?"

"I don't see that it's necessary, but if he needs it for ammo, he might."

"Only you and Sean even know about that. I didn't tell anyone else."

"Why, honey, I'm honored," Megan said softly. "I've not had a lot of time to keep in touch with close friends except some of the girls back in Missouri, and I enjoy our girl time. Hey, is it true that Gerard caught your lip color on Sean's mouth when you two returned from the beach today?"

"Apparently. Leave it to Gerard."

Megan raised the lever to lower the footrest of the recliner, then she strolled across the carpet to the sofa to sit beside Tess and curled her legs beneath her. "I think this might be a night for marshmallow roasting over the fire."

"After we put our pajamas on?"

"We've got to get comfortable so that when our sugar high tanks, we'll be ready for bed."

"You'd do that for me?"

Megan giggled. "Just for you."

"Since you're my bodyguard right now, why don't we take a road trip tomorrow? Maybe turn our cell phones off, hit some waves, play with the bullet fish and dolphins?"

"Try out some new seafood restaurant?"

"Maybe you can take some extra days off for the next two weeks, find some kind docs to volunteer at the clinic. I want to take a break before Christmas."

"From everything?"

"Everything."

"Even Sean?"

"Especially Sean."

"You trying to break his heart?"

"No, I'm giving us both some distance. He needs room to do whatever he needs to do, and I need to tune out."

"I'll check with Gerard about some time off."

Tess was surprised by the rush of relief Megan's words gave her. She'd never had a sister, but she suspected this must be what it felt like. Warm. Safe. Comfortable.

NINE

At nine a.m. on Christmas Eve, Sean entered through the back door of the mission after another successful news report over the air. There'd been no more deaths or illnesses for two weeks, and he was getting a little jittery. It had been two weeks between Carlotta's death and Stud's poisoning. Tomorrow was Christmas. If the killer was going to make another move, the time may be ripe for it.

But Sean hoped his maneuver had worked. The day after his argument with Tess, he had, indeed, announced that Tess had withdrawn from Corpus Christi, and why. She was answering no phones, she wasn't coming into the mission, and Gerard had moved Colleen from the store to take on admin duties. Both Tess's cell and Gerard's landline phones had been on hiatus.

Someone was, of course, still doing the work that only Tess had been able to do—promotion, publicity, keeping the mission in the public eye. Sean was definitely doing his part. Every few days he had something new to announce over the air about the incident in Austin and the health of the poisoning victims at the mission.

Business at the store had increased for both incoming items and sales, and donations were up over last Christmas by a wide margin. The smear campaign had failed.

Gerard met Sean at the downstairs door to the admin stairwell. He held his finger to his lips and nodded toward the back door. "Let's take another walk."

"Same course?"

"Let's go the other direction. Keep our spooks guessing."

They fell into step together across the customer parking lot, same pace as before. "I miss Tess," Sean said.

"She's moping around the house like a lost kitten."

"Good."

"What a loving thing to say."

"I'm just saying she's not exactly in the witness protection program."

"But for everyone's safety, she's pretending she is."

"I want to drive to the ranch and see her."

"Not yet."

"When?"

"Soon."

"That's what you've said the past five times I've asked. You know she and I have never cleared up this misunderstanding between us."

"More time just means the making up will be sweeter."

"How do you know?"

"Have you forgotten I was engaged?"

"Oh. Yeah." Sean felt it wise not to remind his friend that the engagement had been broken.

Gerard glanced over his shoulder when they were a block from the mission. "I called for a bug scan two weeks ago, but the company has been busy. Jim came in last night, swept everything quietly. Found one bug. It was attached to the bottom of Tess's office door."

"Any fingerprints on it?"

"A couple of partials. It's being run through a database now, but Sugar McCrae has no priors, so now she'll have to be picked up and fingerprinted."

They walked another full block while Sean processed the information. "No guarantees, but it's possible that's what the intruder was doing upstairs two weeks ago, the night before the poisoning."

"And the intruder would be the poisoner. Evidence of that

is with the lab in the form of the arsenic footprint. I've been rechecking some of the backgrounds we did on Tess's former employees, someone who might have held a grudge, especially Emil Mason, the embezzler."

"Isn't he still in prison?"

"He is, but I put in a call to do a complete background check on Sugar—aka Sherleen—McCrae. Got my answer back this morning. She's Emil's illegitimate half sister."

"Whoa. How did you find that out?"

"The father was listed on the birth certificate."

"You think Emil and Sugar knew each other?"

"Seems probable, considering."

"Okay then, I might believe she's holding a grudge against Tess because Tess saw to it that her brother was prosecuted," Sean said, "but to commit murder?"

"We've seen that kind before. Psychotic. She's obviously unstable enough to risk her reputation by giving bad info."

"Yes, but—"

"I know. It's a far cry from murder. I'm still putting some pieces together. For instance, I'm curious why Channel Eleven didn't say anything about the notes Tess received."

"The culprit wouldn't share the information about the notes because she wouldn't want to clear her victim. Have you found any evidence that McCrae's still in Corpus Christi?"

"As of yesterday, she was trying to pawn more of her faulty tips off on Channel Six. They weren't interested."

"If she's still here, and if she's serious enough to commit murder, don't you think it's possible she's still watching for Tess to return to the mission?"

"But Tess isn't going to return."

"And if we never catch her stalker? Is she going to hide out at your house for the rest of her life?"

"We'll find her stalker."

"I hope so, because I can't see Tess giving up the rest of her life because she's afraid of losing it."

"I already told Captain Clark our suspicions about Sugar

McCrae. When they find her they'll have plenty of evidence to hold her for questioning."

"Now, all we have to do is wait."

Tess sat in her home office and tried to tally a final page of numbers. They didn't match. She searched through a stack of receipts but couldn't find those that supported the heftiest numbers on the expense report. And she knew where the receipts were—somewhere in her office at the mission. And she needed them right now. She had to have this report wrapped up and delivered to their accountant today for year-end audits.

She groaned and buried her face in her hands. Roxie looked up from her perch beside the desk and whined.

"It's okay, girl. I just have to go undercover for a trip to town." Against all of her better judgment. Against Gerard's strict commands. The IRS could not be kept waiting.

Twenty minutes later, wearing Gerard's brown hooded sweatshirt, some old sunglasses and her baggiest pair of jeans, she drove the farm truck into the customer parking lot and entered the mission through the front of the store.

No one called out to her. No one recognized her. She began to relax.

Gerard would kill her for this. But Gerard wouldn't be happy if they were audited by the IRS, either. Her office door was locked when she reached it. She knocked, and there was no answer, so she used her key, slipped inside and found the receipts she needed in the one filing drawer Gerard hadn't emptied and taken to the ranch.

Why had she waited until today to gather everything together? Wasn't she stressed enough without having this to worry about?

She placed everything into an accordion file and closed the drawer, turned to leave the office and ran headlong into Sean's hard chest. She stumbled backward.

"Tess?" He reached out to steady her. "What are you—"

"Oh, no! Don't tell Gerard you saw me, or he'll make me eat liver and parsnips for a week."

"He's not here, but this time I'm not making any promises. You're not supposed to be here."

"I'm maintaining telephone silence, and I need these papers today. Deadline. No choice."

"You're maintaining telephone silence, yet you're walking in here yourself? At what level does that make sense?"

"At the level of phone tapping."

"As opposed to the possibility of someone actually seeing you walk in here?"

"Nobody but you recognized me." She tugged at the hood she'd pulled from her head and the glasses she'd removed after entering the office. "I drove the farm truck, and Gerard has never driven it to town. No one here knows what it looks like."

Sean glanced at the windows and stepped over to close the blinds. "Gerard told you about the bug that was found on the bottom of your door last night?"

"He told me. Apparently Sugar McCrae is a multitalented villain. She uses a car as a weapon, she uses words as weapons, she uses arsenic as a weapon."

Sean closed the door. "Now that you're here—"

"Sean, I have to get back to the ranch. I really do have to get these papers into the packet for our accountant."

"How long will that take? Five minutes? You have time to talk to me."

Tess glanced at the clock on the wall. "Okay. You're right. We're only looking at a possible audit by the IRS. No big deal."

"We carry insurance with the accounting firm for just such an incident. I can even drive out to the ranch and help you complete the report if you want."

"Wow, you really want to talk, don't you?" She placed the accordion file on the desk and sat next to it. Colleen kept a tidier desk than she did. "Where's Gerard?"

"Police station. Our suspect has been apprehended and is being held for twenty-four hours. He's not doing any questioning, of course, but he wants to follow their movements until he can be sure Sugar McCrae is guilty of murder."

"Okay, sorry I asked. It seems all I've thought about these past few days is what that woman has done." She looked at Sean, who sat on top of the two-drawer filing cabinet. Their knees almost touched.

"Then we won't talk about her," Sean said. "I've missed you, Tess. Gerard seems to think a good lovers' quarrel helps clear the air every so often, but I didn't remind him his engagement didn't work out."

"Wise move. Sean, we're not lovers."

"We're friends who love each other. That makes us lovers."

Tess thought about that.

"And I'm sorry I betrayed you," Sean said. "I was sorry when I was doing it. I hated it, but I would do it again under the same circumstances."

"So, does this mean I can never confide in you anymore, because you might betray me over the radio?"

"I've been praying it never comes to that again."

She frowned at him.

"Tess, you can trust me with your secrets."

She met his gaze and held it for a long moment. For the time being, it was just the two of them in the office. No one else existed. "I believe you."

"If we find out Sugar McCrae is your stalker, will you start answering my calls again?"

"I haven't given much thought to what I'd do, because I never thought the killer would be found after all this time. I honestly thought I might have to evade her for the rest of my life. And thanks for bringing up that subject yet again."

"I wouldn't let you be stalked for the rest of your life," he said softly. "Do you know why I work so much here at the mission?"

"It's your way of protecting the most vulnerable."

"That's one reason. I started helping out before the abortion so Gerard could protect you. I started working here again after the abortion because of guilt. I kept working here because it's something I feel called to do and I've never known such satisfaction before. But I also wonder from time to time if the biggest draw is the fact that you're here and I just can't bear to be away from you. Not quite as noble a reason for being here, is it?"

His words finally filled that void she'd felt since their fight. She'd been raw for two weeks, and all of a sudden she felt as if those raw spots had healed.

"For the past eight months," Sean said, "I've felt that I had no right to a deeper relationship with any woman, especially not a woman as strong and compassionate and loyal as you are. But I've had some talks with Gerard lately, and as Gerard has explained, I needed to learn how to live without my old rusty set of rules. I had to forgive myself."

"Sean, you're forgiven."

"Except I had trouble forgiving Kari Ann. I haven't been able to move forward because of that until last week, when I took a long walk and prayed for help."

"Have you forgiven her now?"

"I've found it's a process. I can let it go, forgive her, put it out of my mind, and then when I think of it again, the anger is back."

"You've got to get points for the attempts. It gets easier the more often you do it. I don't even know who I'm supposed to forgive. My enemy is still out there. And I still have trouble forgiving myself for letting physical attraction bind me to the wrong man. I've asked myself several times since our disagreement whether I'm even capable of sustaining a relationship. That's something I never told you before."

"You're capable, Tess. You've always been a devoted sister and daughter. You've been true to yourself and your future husband by remaining pure. I don't know a lot of people who would be more capable of sustaining a long and happy marriage. Look at your parents. What a beautiful example."

"Our fight scared me."

"Yeah, I know."

"Didn't it scare you?"

"Not really. It frustrated me, but I know you, Tess. You're a forgiving person. Honestly, you've had Gerard as a brother for thirty-two years; I have no doubt about your ability to forgive."

She knew he was trying to get her to smile, to laugh, but she couldn't. "Fighting with you broke my heart. I hate that."

"Your heart didn't break, it was bruised. You're tough. You can handle this. I have no doubt at all that you'll be able to maintain a good relationship when you realize who the right man is."

Tess swallowed. "I've already done that."

He leaned back with a grin. "See? I told you I knew you loved me."

"What makes you think it's you?"

His cocky grin vaporized.

She laughed and reached for her accordion file. "Now, I have to get this paperwork to the accountant."

As she slid from the desk, Sean stood up and reached for her. "Okay, one more shared secret before you leave."

"Are you sure you want to do this?" she asked. "Because I know some of your employees, and I'm not above retaliation."

"My employees are frightened of me."

"Then what's the secret?"

"I know this sounds like a pickup line, but I suspected I was in trouble from the moment I first met you. After I got to know you, there was no longer any doubt. Now, don't laugh again, but for the longest time, while you were building your career and getting yourself engaged, I was making friends in bars."

"And fending off women, no doubt."

He shrugged. "Maybe sometimes."

"Don't give me that. You have a mirror. You had women flocking to meet you. I bet they wondered what a hunk like you was doing still single at thirty-six."

"You think I'm a hunk?"

"So are my brothers, so don't take it personally. What did you tell the curious women?"

"I just told them I was waiting for the woman of my dreams to grow up and realize I was the one she loved."

"And now that she has?"

That slow grin spread once more across his face. He took the accordion file from her arms and placed it back on the desk, drew her into his arms and kissed her. She could almost hear the cries of seagulls and catch the scent of the gulf breeze.

TEN

Sean opened the blinds in Tess's office and watched out the window as she pulled out of the customer parking lot in Gerard's big farm truck with rattling sideboards. According to Gerard, she had learned to drive in that truck when she was twelve, and she could shift the gears like a pro.

He stood in that window long after she had disappeared from sight, realizing just what his heart had gotten him into when he fell in love with her. Not only was she independent and strong, but she never stopped surprising him. He could spend a lifetime with her and the excitement would never end. Ever.

His cell phone rang when he was walking into his own office. It was Gerard.

"Sugar McCrae's the one who ran the smear campaign, all right," Gerard said. "Problem is she's got an airtight alibi for the night before. She works as a bartender at Cooper's on the bay, doesn't get off until the wee morning hours. The prints lifted from the bug don't match hers. She also has an alibi for the night Tanner was killed."

"Which is?"

"She's been a bartender at Cooper's for three years. She was working that night, too."

"Is she still being questioned?"

"Yes, and now it's getting interesting. She's apparently been watching the mission since she saw Tess at our store one day.

She shops there a lot. She was still angry with Tess for putting her brother away, and she was looking for something she could do for payback. While watching, she just happened to see someone else watching the mission from the upstairs studio apartment across the street. There appeared to be a telescope."

"Man or woman?"

"Woman. Short, brown hair. Sugar saw her two or three times. Always in the daytime. She never saw the woman go inside the mission, but Sugar wasn't usually around at night because of her job. The apartment she described is directly across from Tess's office. With a telescope, whoever was watching could see Tess whenever she was in there."

Sean studied the windows across the street. The shade over the far window was open, but he couldn't see anyone. "Gerard, someone needs to search the apartment now. Tess just left."

"What? You have got to be kidding me. Why on earth would she do—"

"She needed backup papers for the accountant. She wore your clothes, drove your truck, nobody knew her when she came in. I caught her when I came upstairs, but the blinds were open. I closed them, but if anyone was watching they'd have seen her with her hood down and glasses off. Could even be following her now."

"I'll get the police over there."

"I'll call the ranch and tell the hands not to allow anyone to follow Tess to the house." He lowered the blind. "I'm on my way out now."

"Meet you there." Gerard clicked off.

Sean raced through the mission and out to his truck, calling the ranch as he ran.

When Tess slowed to turn at the gate to the ranch, Morty Snyder, Gerard's foreman, walked out with his hands held out for her to stop.

She rolled down the window with difficulty. "Hey, what's up?"

"I got two calls telling me to check the house, wave you

down, check the truck and make sure no one's following you." He nudged the open flap of his jacket aside to show he was carrying a sidearm. "High alert, let me tell you. They're racing out here now."

"Did they say why all the excitement?"

"Said Sugar McCrae's innocent of everything but malicious gossip, but somebody's been watching your office, may've seen you at the mission today. Anybody follow you?"

"Nope, I kept an eye on the rearview mirror, even took a few unnecessary turns."

"The dogs have been in the yard all the time you've been gone, and they didn't kick up a fuss once, so no stranger's been there. I walked around the house. It's all locked up tight. No one's been down this road since you left. Let me check the truck, and you can be on your way."

"Thanks, Morty. I guess this one's a false alarm. Would you call Gerard and tell him? I'll call Sean." She rolled her window up and waited for him to check the back and wave her on.

She turned her cell phone on for the first time in two weeks, hit speed dial and reached Sean. "Hold your horses, speed demon," she said when he answered. "No one followed me. You can turn around and go back to town."

"Not happening."

"You really think I'm in danger right this minute? Morty even checked the back of the truck, and there's no one there."

"How about behind the seat?"

"Well, no." Despite her assurances to Sean, Tess felt a frisson of tension across her shoulders. "But Gerard has all his tools back there, and nobody could fit. Besides, who's going to try to crawl into a hiding place in the middle of the day on a busy street?"

"A crazy person determined to get to you."

"That isn't what I wanted to hear."

"Just keep driving and get into the house. Take the dogs inside with you. I'll be there in ten minutes, maybe less."

"I'll see you when you get here."

"Don't disconnect. Press the speaker button and put your phone in your pocket. You're carrying your mace, aren't you?"

"Sure am."

"Get it out and carry it in your hand."

She reached into her purse and pulled out the house keys and mace as she parked the truck at the side of the house. "The dogs are running to the fence, relaxed and happy. I don't think there's a problem here. See you in a few." She did as she was told and left the phone open in the pocket of Gerard's jacket.

"Hey, kids, have you been on guard?" She opened the front gate and knelt down to hug Romper and Roxie to her. "Let's go inside for a while, shall we?"

Since moving in with Gerard, Tess seldom used the front door because she always parked in the garage. Fumbling with several keys, she stuck her mace into the pocket with her cell phone while she unlocked and opened the door.

The dogs rushed in ahead of her, nearly knocking her against the threshold. "Hey, would you two remember your manners?"

Without waiting for her, they ran toward the kitchen. They must be hungry.

Keys still jingling in her hands, she locked the door behind her, turned the dead bolt, glanced out the window to make sure all was in order outside. It was.

She swung around to catch up with the dogs and give them a treat. And she gasped. A woman with short, dark brown hair stood in the hallway connecting the living room to the kitchen. She had a silenced semiautomatic in her hand.

"Kari Ann?"

"You know, those dogs are amazing." Gone was the long, blond hair, the heavy makeup, the elegant clothing Kari Ann Jennings had always worn when she was with Sean. "They remembered me from Christmas last year. Didn't make a peep when I came in the backyard."

"How did you get in here?"

"How do you think?" the woman snapped. "A key."

"What did you do, lift a key from Sean's pocket and make copies while he was sleeping?"

Kari Ann raised an eyebrow. "Maybe you're not as stupid as I thought. Ugly and selfish and vile, but at least you have a brain."

"How did you get here?"

"Did you really think you could get away with what you did? Engaged to one man, sleeping with another?"

"I've never slept with—"

"Save your lies for someone who's fooled. Sean, maybe. Does he still think you're a perfect angel?"

"You obviously didn't drive. And I don't think you hitched a ride with me."

"You think the driveway's the only way to get here? Ever heard of hiking?" Kari Ann narrowed her eyes and studied Tess's body. "Probably not. You're such a busy lady. No, wait, make that busy broad. You're no lady."

Tess knew she should keep her mouth shut and respect the weapon in this crazy woman's hand, but she felt her temper rising. This crazy woman had killed Tanner. This crazy woman had poisoned innocent people out of spite. And now she fully intended to kill again.

Tess could reach into her pocket and pull out her mace, but what good was mace against a Glock already aimed at her heart?

Kari Ann studied Tess's face closely and gave a harsh, humorless laugh. "You're not escaping this time."

"What did you do to the dogs?"

"Fed them."

"Poison?"

Kari Ann gave her a grim smile. "Would that break your heart? Oh, no, wait, you don't have a heart. You like to steal men from their women."

Tess suddenly realized Sean was listening to this whole conversation. Stall. Distract. Keep her talking.

"I don't know what gave you the idea I stole your man. I was engaged to Tanner Jackson until you killed him."

"I could've been engaged to Sean Torrance if you hadn't seduced him."

"Seduced him?"

"He went to you in Austin instead of spending his time off with me. I saw him. Don't deny it."

"If you're talking about those times he went to Austin to guard me, haven't you been listening to his radio reports lately? He did that in response to your notes. How does it feel to know that your threats were what brought him to my side to protect me from—"

"Stop it! Just shut up!"

"Would you have done it if you'd known your notes were the reason you lost him, Kari Ann?"

The woman's hands shook, and Tess held her breath, frozen, as she waited for a blast. She'd pushed too far.

"He can't protect you now, can he?" Kari Ann's voice trembled.

Tess saw movement out the back window in the kitchen, just past Kari Ann's shoulder. Sean. She had to distract this crazy woman.

"And how does it feel to know you were supposed to die instead of Tanner?" Kari Ann asked.

"Neither of us was supposed to die. You're the one who killed him." Keep talking. Sean was coming through the back door. "You're the one who broke into the admin offices to attach a bug to the bottom of my door so you could keep tabs on me, but you made a mistake. You left a footprint on the floor and a fingerprint on the bug. The police already know all about you."

Kari Ann pulled the slider back on her Glock. "Then one more death doesn't matter, does it?"

Tess could see Sean rushing silently through the kitchen to the hallway behind Kari Ann. "You aren't laying any blame at my feet, because I didn't do anything wrong. You were eaten up with jealousy over nothing."

"Liar. I saw the way he watched you, even at Christmas. He listened to your every word, laughed at your lame jokes. I'm prettier than you, I knew I could get his attention, but you kept pulling him away. Anytime he saw you, he couldn't keep his eyes off you, couldn't stop talking about you when we were together."

Sean was in the room, behind Kari Ann. He nodded to Tess, and she dropped to the floor while he grabbed Kari Ann. The pistol went flying, and Kari Ann shrieked her fury as she fought Sean.

Tess snatched up the pistol and checked it, braced herself, got into shooting position.

An engine roared up outside, a door slammed, and Tess backed to the door to unlock it for Gerard.

The two men subdued Kari Ann as she shouted obscenities at Tess. She'd wanted Tess dead since she'd written that first note and finally had decided she would do it herself.

Gerard handcuffed Kari Ann and had her ready for the sheriff when he arrived.

Sean took Tess away from the commotion. They released the dogs from the basement where Kari Ann had lured them and then walked out the back door.

Sean kept his arm around her, as if he couldn't bear to let her go.

"It's over, Tess."

She couldn't speak. She curled herself against Sean's chest and leaned against him.

"It's okay," he said softly. He pressed his lips to her forehead, then to her cheeks, then wrapped his arms so tightly around her she could barely breathe.

"I was so afraid she'd hurt you before I could get here," he whispered. "Oh, Tess, I can't lose you. I love you. You're my heart, my life."

Tears slid down her cheeks, and she nodded.

He held her away from him and looked down at her. "You're safe, Tess. You don't have anything to fear now."

She swallowed. "But you might."

He touched her face with his fingers as if to reassure himself she was really there. "What do you mean?"

"Because I love you with everything in me, and people I love always suffer for it."

"I'll take my chances, Tess. I'll take those chances for the rest of my life if I can spend it with you."

She reached up and combed her fingers through his hair, then pulled him to her until their lips fit together perfectly. It seemed that maybe God really had made this man just for her.

* * * * *

Dear Reader,

Several months ago I met a lady who lives in Hollywood and is engaged in helping the homeless. Her story about what she's seen—whole families living in their cars, on the street, more children and more teens than she's ever seen before—was heartbreaking. These newbies haven't been on the street long and are only there because of recent histories of lost jobs and lost mortgages. They don't know how to fend for themselves.

There are shelters for many of the homeless—for those who wish to abide by the safety rules. Those who do can find food and warmth. Many churches volunteer and trade off working in places of safety. My friends and I purchased items we believed people living on the street might need: small, light foodstuffs, small soaps, toothbrushes and small toothpaste tubes, washcloths, feminine care for women, easy-to-carry toys for children. We sent books, of course, and my friend Marty Frost sent prayer pillows she had made with passages from the Bible written on them. We didn't feel it was enough, but we did what we could.

I began to wonder how I would fare out in the cold with nothing to eat, no place to sleep, and my imagination took hold. I decided to set a romantic suspense at a fictitious homeless shelter, where the people who sought help were well cared for, found medical care, food and were put to work to earn their keep. That's where Vance Mission emerged.

I've seen homeless on the streets in the big cities. It's hard to meet their eyes, especially when I know they're going to be cold later, but that if I give them money, it may well go to drugs and alcohol, not food or the things their bodies really need.

Please consider sending money to a worthy homeless mission for Christmas, maybe even volunteering at a shelter. Treat every kind of human on the street with kindness, because no matter how they ended up where they are, God loves them.

They may have family somewhere who love them. Let's find a productive way to love them, too.

With much love,

Hannah Alexander

Questions for Discussion

1. Tess is a strong woman who was raised in a family of faith, but when she began her own career, she was drawn away from her relationship with God. I think this happens to us all from time to time. When has it happened to you? How were you drawn back?

2. Sean was not raised in a Christian family and was brought to his knees when the woman he got pregnant aborted his child. He went to his friend, Gerard, for counsel, and Gerard led him to faith. Have you ever had an opportunity to gently guide a friend through a crisis? Describe.

3. Tess blames herself for the murder of her fiancé, even though she wasn't the one who murdered him. How would you feel if someone hurt someone you loved to have revenge on you? What would your response be? What should it be?

4. Sean is an ex-cop who carries a weapon, even though he no longer works for the police force. Do you feel he would be innocent if he were to use his weapon to protect himself or others from murder or rape? What if you were called on to protect others? What would go through your mind at that last moment?

5. At one point in the book, Tess seeks the solace of animals in the barn at her brother's ranch. Have you ever found solace in the presence of a dog, a cat, a horse? Please describe such a time.

6. What goes through your mind when you see someone on the street pushing a shopping cart or carrying a black

plastic bag, dirty, with eyes cast down? What are some of the emotions you feel?

7. Tess and Sean both often feel helpless in the face of all the needs at the mission. Do you sometimes feel overwhelmed when you can't meet your own expectations or those of others? Do you feel it's a sin to learn to say no? Have you learned that word yet? How can you practice it during the day?

8. In this story, true love wins out. It doesn't always happen that way, and even Christians who are taught to be gentle and turn the other cheek have temper problems and relationship difficulties. What are some of the ways we can get around those difficulties?

MISTLETOE MAYHEM

Jill Elizabeth Nelson

To pet-lovers and people-lovers all over the world.
May the love of Christ shine through your life!

Words kill, words give life;
They're either poison or fruit—you choose.
—*Proverbs* 18:21

ONE

Kelly Granger stared into Nick Milton's bloodshot eyes and suppressed a shiver. It wouldn't do to betray her fear of him, any more than to give that advantage to a wild animal.

Beefy face taut, Nick leaned toward her over the counter of the veterinary clinic's reception area. "If my dog don't perk up and shake off that drug you pumped into him, I'll come lookin' for you. He's been layin' around all afternoon, worthless as a tick."

His slurred words betrayed the alcohol he pickled himself in daily. How did Chelsea live with this guy?

"Mr. Milton, Brutus's behavior posed a danger to himself, the staff and other animals. In order to give him his checkup and vaccinations, it was necessary to administer a mild sedative first. I assure you, he will be himself by morning, barring a little stiffness in the vaccination site, which will also disappear."

There, she'd delivered a reasonable explanation, and her voice didn't even quiver. If she'd discovered any sign of abuse on Nick's Doberman, she would have turned the dog over to the SPCA to get the animal away from his disgusting owner.

"Highfalutin, la-di-da doctor!" Nick shook a ham-size fist in her face. "I'm holdin' you to them words."

Kelly gripped the edge of the counter. She would not back away. The creep might have a reputation for temper, but she was *not* going to be cowed. This was *her* clinic, and she'd done nothing wrong…except send her assistant, Tim Hallock, home early. Tim might be half Nick's size, but at least he could have called the cops.

Nick turned and stomped out the door, admitting a burst of chill air, which washed over Kelly. She allowed herself a shiver. Some people needed a muzzle and leash more than their pets. She wouldn't mind calling the police to let them know Nick Milton was driving drunk again, except he wasn't driving.

The Milton's beat-up van sat in a parking spot outside the clinic's picture window. Nick's son, Greg, perched behind the wheel. Kelly's glance met the teenager's, and the kid offered his usual juvenile leer. She marched to the door and turned the deadbolt as the van chugged out of the parking lot, spewing dark smoke from its tailpipe.

Releasing a breath, she looked out the picture window, which revealed a panorama of white-topped mountain ridges looming over the struggling business district. Even with Christmas nearly upon them, traffic was thin this early evening. Vehicle headlights vied with the twinkle of Christmas lights adorning the facades of the buildings. Thankfully, no one seemed headed for the veterinary clinic. She'd dealt with enough excitement for one day.

Brutus had been the easiest patient—a routine well-check. Six other pets, cradled by distraught owners—one of them Kelly's sister—had been presented this afternoon, each animal exhibiting the same awful symptoms. She was keeping most of them overnight on IVs to rehydrate them. Her patients would live, but more by the grace of God than human skill. She'd never seen anything like it and prayed she never would again.

Had Tim remembered to prepare the biological samples for submission to the state lab? They needed to discover what had made the pets so ill.

Kelly headed for the pharmacy, loafers squeaking faintly on the linoleum. Her pharmacy was more like a large closet than a room. The package lay wrapped and labeled on the counter. Kelly smiled. Reliable was Tim's middle name.

A note in his handwriting sat by the box. She picked it up and read, "Courier service unable to make the pick-up until *late* tomorrow afternoon. One of the hazards of living in a Tennessee mountain town."

Kelly groaned. Compared to the frenzy of her Nashville vet school experience, she'd loved returning to the gracious pace of life in Abbottsville, nestled in the heart of the Great Smoky Mountains. But around here, tomorrow was soon enough for anything to happen. Might as well get home and put her feet up.

On the drive to her modest bungalow, her thoughts refused to wind down. What if the illness was an epidemic—something bacterial...or even viral? Or maybe it was as simple as a contaminated batch of pet food? But what if this was a contagion that could infect people? What if... *Whoa, girl!* No point in stressing over what had hit the pets of Abbottsville until the lab returned results.

Darkness had fully fallen when she turned the final corner onto her street. She accelerated and then eased off on the gas pedal. What was up with this? The automatic timer on her Christmas lights should have had her place aglow with festive decorations, but the single-story home was dark. A faulty timer? Better that than some expensive electrical issue. It wasn't a power outage. The porch light glowed on the two-story house next door, but no holiday decorations. Probably because her yet-to-be-seen neighbor had moved in only yesterday.

Kelly wheeled the Explorer into her driveway, and the headlights passed over a scene of Christmas decoration carnage strewn across her snow-dusted lawn. What in the world? She halted the SUV at an angle and scanned the mess of tinsel, strings of lights, straw from the creche and holly and pine garland. Her stomach knotted. Who would do such a thing? Then she spotted the vandal, and her jaw dropped.

The big, hairy culprit sat tall and proud on the cement step by her front door. Leaving the lights on, Kelly put the vehicle in Park and hopped out. Hands on hips, she studied the half-grown Saint Bernard pup. She'd never seen this fellow before. Whose was he? He wore a collar and tag, so he wasn't a stray. Was he friendly?

One way to find out. Kelly stepped toward the dog. The animal rose to all fours, tongue lolling, and wagged his tail so hard his thick haunches swayed back and forth. Guess that answered her question.

"What a naughty boy you've been!" Kelly's soft tone contradicted the scold.

Whoof! The dog lunged toward her. Enormous paws thumped against her chest, and Kelly's *whoof* echoed the dog's bark. His tongue stroked the bottom of her chin. Keeping her balance—barely—she pushed the animal away, then bent and grabbed his collar.

"Down, boy." His hot, wet tongue anointed her cheek. Friendly didn't begin to describe this pup. "Hasn't anyone taught you manners?"

Whew! Another six months, and this guy would be able to land his paws on top of her shoulders and look her square in the eye while he bathed her face. Whoever owned the animal needed to get him better trained before then.

"Ben! You big doofus! What have you done this time?"

The deep voice brought Kelly's head up to see a tall, lean man trot down the porch steps of the house next door, cell phone clutched in his fist. He wore jeans and a long-sleeved, button-down shirt, and his head was crowned with blond hair so pale it gleamed nearly white in the beams of her car headlights. The strong, unlined features beneath the thick hair indicated he was in his early- to mid-thirties, not much older than her, newly thirty.

The pup barked, broke away from Kelly and galumphed toward his master. At least, she assumed this must be the owner of the sweet-natured mischief-maker. Who could stay angry at such a cute dog? And the rest of the mess on her lawn? Well, the pup was doing what came naturally. Now, the negligent owner—him, she could blame.

The man bent and ruffled the fur around the dog's neck while issuing affectionate scolds.

Frowning, Kelly crossed her arms. "Your dog is adorable, but while you were yakking on the phone, he made mincemeat of my Christmas decorations."

The man fixed his gaze on Kelly. She couldn't tell the color of his eyes, even in the glow of her headlights, but the intensity of the look sent a surge to her pulse.

"Matthew Bennett." He rose to his full height, at least half a head taller than her five foot seven, and stepped forward, extending his hand. "You'd better call me Matt, since it looks like we're neighbors."

She accepted a handshake, his generous palm warm against her cold fingers. "Kelly Granger," she muttered, willing herself not to check for a wedding ring.

"I'm sorry you had to meet Ben and me this way. Not the first impression I'd prefer to make." A grin put attractive dents in his cheeks. "Let me take this bad boy to the house and grab a jacket. Then I'll come back and clean up."

Kelly glanced around at the disaster. "We can't leave it to blow through the neighborhood overnight. I'd better help sort through things to see what's salvageable."

"Sure. I'll be right back." Man and dog trotted toward their house.

Groaning, Kelly plodded to her front door. Inside, she removed her shoes and headed in stocking feet to her Spartan kitchen. Cooking didn't number among her interests. That was her sister's forte, and Kelly generally ate at Brenda's restaurant. Tonight her appetite had been stolen, and she craved nothing more than the three *B*s—bath, book and bed. Instead, she had a cleanup job to tackle. She yanked open a drawer and grabbed a flashlight. The car headlights didn't illuminate the whole lawn, and she'd need something to pierce the shadows.

She returned to the wintry yard to find Matt whistling a holiday tune beneath his breath while he stuffed shreds of tinsel into a garbage bag. Kelly gritted her teeth. Why hadn't she thought to bring a bag?

"Here you go." He grinned and held out a square of black plastic.

"Thank you." She snatched the bag.

This guy's strong dose of cheerful when she'd rather spit a few nails was almost too much to take, but her mama had raised her to be a lady, and ladies are always polite. She migrated to a dark segment of yard on the other side of the walk from her handsome nemesis neighbor and clicked on her flashlight. The beam fell on a mound of debris.

A scream left her throat. "My wreath!"

"Oh, man." Matt rustled up beside her. "Ben did a number on that one. Don't worry. I'll replace everything."

"You don't understand!" Kelly rounded on him, nostrils flaring. If the top of her head could pop off, it might release actual steam. "The mistletoe wreath was an heirloom handed down for generations." She smacked her arms against her sides. "I paid a bundle to have it refurbished and professionally preserved so I could hang it on my front door, and now look at it! All because you couldn't keep track of your dog. Pet owners have got to be more responsible!"

A lump formed in her throat. Why had she not noticed that the wreath was missing from the door? Enough was plain enough! She thrust the garbage bag at her openmouthed neighbor and fled into the house.

Tears bathed her cheeks as she slid her back down the panel until her seat met the polished wood floor. What a foolish reaction to the loss of a Christmas decoration—heirloom or not. But she had so little of her heritage to treasure. With her parents gone in a car accident five years ago, she and her sister were the last twigs on the family tree.

But Matt couldn't know that. He must think she was a nut job. Not a great impression to make on the most interesting guy she'd met since Blake decided to take his engagement ring back. Kelly's heart shriveled, and her jaw firmed.

"You're not in the market." She spoke out loud to herself. "Who cares if the new neighbor has cute dimples? Looks are skin-deep."

Matt stood holding the bag—actually two bags—and studied Kelly Granger's closed door. He'd shot himself in the foot with his beautiful neighbor.

Shaking his head, he finished picking up the debris from the yard. There wasn't much salvageable, least of all the heirloom mistletoe wreath. Kelly had been right. He needed to get that dog into a training class, but his life had been too hectic with emergencies in his job of state health inspector and the move from Nashville to this remote area. He'd hoped the smaller community would afford him peace and quiet during what little downtime his career afforded. What a way to begin!

Later, Matt sat in his easy chair in front of a snapping blaze in the fireplace and scratched behind Ben's ears while the pup snoozed on the floor. The ruddy hue that edged the golden flames reminded him of his neighbor's vibrant hair. He'd never been partial to redheads, so why this woman should stick in his brain, he didn't know. But when he'd seen the look on her face as she'd gazed at her destroyed wreath, his arms had ached to hold her and absorb some of her pain.

The appealing picture of her leaning into him, bright head on his shoulder, took form in his mind's eye. Matt hissed in a breath. He must really be bushed to let his imagination take off on him like that. Sure, he'd moved to Abbottsville as the outward symbol of his inner decision that he was ready to move on since the loss of his wife. Four years was long enough to grieve, wasn't it? Sometimes he thought so. Other times, at the oddest moments, pain twisted his guts as though the funeral was yesterday.

Matt waved a hand in front of his face as if dispelling smoke. Time to hit the hay. As he rose, his cell phone rang from the side table. He grabbed it, then frowned. The central office calling at this hour?

"Bennett here."

"Matt, you've got an assignment for ASAP in the morning." It was Will Jessup, his boss.

"Where am I headed this time?" Great! Not even forty-eight hours to settle in.

"Your own new backyard. Five residents of Abbottsville have been hospitalized with symptoms of an illness that could be food poisoning. Our victims patronized Brenda's Kitchen within the past twenty-four hours. Collect samples from the restaurant and get them to the lab right away."

"That serious, huh?" A chill spread through Matt. Most food poisoning patients were treated and sent home to recuperate. Only severe cases were hospitalized. In this instance, since Abbottsville didn't have a hospital, they would have been transported to Sevierville, the county seat. "Do you want me to close the restaurant?"

"Not until the lab confirms a food-borne agent rather than simply some variation of the flu. We should know before the end of the day tomorrow, and then we'll have the clout to close."

Matt snapped his phone shut on a groan. His neighbor couldn't stand him, and now he could mess up his rapport with the rest of the town by investigating a restaurant in Abbottsville. But the alternative was unacceptable—more people falling ill, potentially dying. Well, if worst came to worst, and the town hated his guts because of his job, he could always relocate. Again.

At 5:58 a.m., Matt pulled into a parking space across the street from the main restaurant in town, Brenda's Kitchen. The stone-and-timber establishment was located on the north end of the one-thoroughfare business district. The structure was well-maintained, but looked like it had stood sentry on this spot since dirt was created. Numerous pickups and cars idled outside, exhaust fogging the darkness. Promptly at 6:00 a.m., the Open light came on in the window.

Matt hefted his bulky kit and stepped into the winter morning. When the sun came up, temps should reach into the low forties, but right now, he was glad for his down-filled jacket. The staccato clamor of slamming car doors echoed in the predawn gloom. His breath painted white trails in the air as he joined a surge of patrons who jostled and joshed and called, "Merry Christmas," like they'd known each other since the building had been constructed.

Yeasty, savory smells welcomed them, and the patrons dispersed to quaintly dated booths and tables, much like folks on Sunday morning beelining for their favorite pews. Perfect—on his second day of residency in Abbottsville, he had to approach the owner of what amounted to a community landmark with the dreaded *E* phrase on his lips—suspicion of e. coli.

Matt approached the cash register and set his testing kit at his feet. The black bag resembled an oversize briefcase and seldom attracted a second glance from patrons. Shortly afterward, a fortyish waitress with a thin build and a strained smile paused in her scurrying.

"Merry Christmas," she said. "Can I help you?"

A pin on her right shoulder identified her as Chelsea. He requested to see the owner or manager and was escorted to the entrance of the kitchen.

"Brenda, someone here to see you." Chelsea grabbed a coffeepot and hustled off.

The cook, a generous-figured woman about his own age and clad in a white apron, turned from the industrial-size griddle. She held gloved hands upright and away from her body almost like a surgeon. Her brown hair was pinned atop her head and encased in a mesh net. She wore little makeup, and her only jewelry was a pink ribbon pin, symbolic of the fight against breast cancer.

"We were inspected two months ago," Brenda said, eyeing his kit.

Matt lifted one corner of his mouth. The details patrons didn't notice about his kit, business owners did. "I'm Matt Bennett from the Tennessee Department of Health. We've got suspicious cases in the area."

Her shoulders slumped. "Come on in and do what's necessary. As you can see, I run a tight ship. I'd better get back at it." She turned toward her griddle and flipped eggs.

Matt went to the massive stainless steel refrigerator. He retrieved his paperwork and clipboard from the kit, as well as sample-gathering containers. Then he donned gloves.

"Brenda, you didn't tell me you hired new kitchen help."

The familiar voice stopped Matt as he reached into the refrigerator. He turned to look into a pair of crystal-green eyes. Kelly stood in the kitchen doorway. Her cool assessment sent tingles to his toes—like a peppermint bath.

Brenda snorted. "Mr. Bennett's from the state health department."

Kelly's eyes narrowed. "I thought you aced your routine inspection."

"We did." Brenda motioned the other woman into the kitchen, darted a sidelong look at Matt, then leaned close to Kelly. "This is *not* routine."

The urgent hiss barely carried to Matt's ears.

Eyes wide, Kelly turned toward him. "You're investigating my sister's establishment for cause?" Her tone was sharp enough to slice warm bread.

Matt looked from Kelly to Brenda and back again. These two were sisters? The only resemblance was the firm, slightly pointed chin. His stomach turned to lead. If he was toast with Kelly Granger yesterday, he was mud today.

"Just doing my job, miss." The flat statement sounded as lame as it felt to his heart.

"Lighten up, Kell," Brenda said. "If folks are getting sick, we need to find out why."

Kelly deflated, but her gaze never left Matt's. "Do you mean symptoms like the stomach flu but it's not the flu?"

Matt nodded. "You'll probably start hearing word around town soon that people have been hospitalized."

Her cheeks paled. "I think you should stop over to my vet clinic. Half a dozen pets came in yesterday with flu-like symptoms. We almost lost a couple of them. Maybe you'd like to send my biological samples in with yours. You'd have a fast track to get them processed."

Matt studied the strong features of the woman who gazed steadily back at him. Slender, straight nose. Full, though not pouty, lips. Eyebrows, dark slashes above those striking eyes. The combination, along with the rich fire of her hair, was arresting.

"I'll come over as soon as I finish here."

His pulse quickened as he watched her walk away. Faded jeans and a long-sleeved flannel shirt resembled designer clothes on her. Maybe this assignment wasn't a total disaster if it gave him an opportunity to spend time with this intriguing woman.

Kelly drove to her clinic in the fresh morning light, kneading the steering wheel. When Matt zeroed those intense blue eyes in on her, she'd almost changed her mind about having him stop by the clinic. Of course, her reluctance for further association stemmed from concern for her sister's business, not the stupid kabump her heart did at the sight of his dimples. But if the pet illnesses were related to the human illnesses, they needed to know as soon as possible, whether or not her annoying neighbor was investigating her sister's restaurant.

Kelly parked in her usual spot behind the clinic. Tim's compact car was already there. She headed toward the rear entrance and frowned. Why was the door ajar? Tim must not have closed it firmly behind him when he opened up.

"Hey, Tim!" She stepped inside and shut the door.

Barks and meows answered from her overnight patients. She hurried toward the convalescent room and then skidded to a halt as she passed an exam room. Her jaw dropped as she stared at a mess that rivaled the disaster on her front lawn last night. Had some wild animal entered through the partially open door? Is that why her patients were going bonkers? Her heart stuttered. Was Tim all right?

Kelly glanced from right to left. No movement. No foreign sounds. The pets had settled into an occasional yip or mewl. Kelly soft-footed toward the convalescent room. Her gaze darted from side to side and spotted more wreckage in the opposite exam area. She pulled her cell phone from her shoulder bag and punched in 9-1-1 by feel.

Scarcely daring to breathe, she peered around the doorframe of the convalescent room. The plastic feeding bucket lay on its side in the middle of the floor, dry pet food strewn around it. The pets in their cages were awake and staring at her.

"Tim?" The word rasped from her throat as barking and meowing gained momentum.

She put the phone to her ear in time to hear a male voice say, "What is the nature of your emergency?"

Kelly opened her mouth, but a wad of cloth cut off her words. An arm encircled her from behind, pinning one of her arms to her side. She flailed backward with the other, and her elbow connected with flesh. Her assailant's grip tightened, squeezing the air from her chest. She lost her hold on the phone, and it skittered across the floor. Instinctively, she inhaled for a scream, and a sweet odor filled her senses. Her mind clouded, her body went slack, and blackness cut off awareness.

TWO

"You and your sister live and work in the same town," Matt commented to Brenda, who bustled around like she was a cross between a honeybee and an ant.

"Born and raised here. Our folks were killed in an accident a while back, so we're all each other have. Except I'm married and have a little girl. My husband, Jerry, is in the service and deployed for the next few months, though. We especially miss him at Christmastime." She sighed. "But he should be home before next Christmas." A smile flickered.

"Being a mom and running a restaurant must keep you busy while you wait," Matt said as he labeled a sample.

"I'm thankful for a healthy little girl and a good business." Brenda bobbed her head. "Kell and I inherited equal shares of the restaurant, but I bought her out so she'd have money to go to veterinary school without borrowing. I thought she'd stay in the city to practice, but she didn't like that atmosphere, so Abbottsville was glad to welcome her home. Her vet office is at the other end of Main." Brenda cranked a thumb in a northward direction. "In fact," she paused in her whirlwind activities, "Kell saved our dog's life last night." Then she pivoted toward the service window. "Order up!"

Brenda continued with her comfortable chatter as Matt worked. He discovered that her little girl, Felice, was three and a half years old and a "real go-getter," and Chelsea, the waitress, was California born and bred but married to a local guy. From the twist of Brenda's lips when she said that last part, Matt inferred she didn't much care for Mr. Local.

Then she asked him a few questions, like where he was from. When he confessed he'd moved in next to Kelly, she rounded on him, eyes narrowed. Her gaze scanned him up and down as though she hadn't really looked at him yet. She gave particular attention to his left hand.

Matt's bare ring finger tingled. He would always miss Carrie, but if he ever hoped to have a family, he had to be open to whoever God might bring into his life. A vision of red hair and green eyes appeared to him. Hah! Like that was a promising prospect after their rough start.

"Hmm." Brenda lifted her brows and went back to work.

Matt blinked. If, by some miracle, he found the opportunity to pursue his interest in Kelly—despite the odds—had he found an ally or an enemy? The answer might depend on what his health investigation revealed.

A door slammed in the back of the restaurant as Chelsea labored into the kitchen, struggling with an overly full tub of dirty dishes. Matt rushed to help her before the whole thing wound up on the floor. The assistance wasn't technically correct, coming from a man in his position, but sometimes common decency needed to overrule the guidebook. He set the heavy tub on the counter near the dishwasher.

Chelsea accepted his help with a smile, then looked beyond him and frowned. "Greg, it's about time. You're late!"

Matt turned to see a medium-tall teenager slouch from the back room into the kitchen, tying an apron around his husky form. The kid scowled, brown bangs half covering one of his downcast eyes. He went straight to the dishes and began loading them into the dishwasher tray. From his looks, he could be related to Chelsea. The waitress muttered more scolds and returned to her customers.

Brenda sent a shrug toward Matt. "Greg is Chelsea's boy. We want our kids to be perfect—for their own good, of course. He must have forgotten to set his alarm again." She said that last sentence loudly enough for Chelsea's son to hear over the dish clatter. "Teenagers need their beauty sleep, eh, Gregster?" The restaurant owner poked her dishwashing help in the arm as she hustled past him toward the pantry.

The kid shrugged, but a grin twitched his thin lips. Brenda had a way with young people. She had a good heart. Matt could only hope that his investigation didn't reveal anything that hurt her.

He started packing up. What might Kelly have to show him at her vet clinic? If the animal illnesses were linked to the human illnesses, then food poisoning might not be the cause. If not, then the list of diseases that could infect both pets and people was pretty narrow, and most of them didn't share the symptoms of food-borne pathogens. Could the problem be traced to some other kind of toxin? That was a scary thought.

He waved toward Brenda and received a brief nod as she put another order up. Greg whipped his head around, and Matt got a look at his right eye. Either the kid had walked into a lamp-post, or someone had slugged him. Fistfight between peers or trouble at home? The question played across Matt's mind as he left the restaurant in search of Kelly's vet clinic.

He studied the town as he drove the length of the main street. Abbottsville might not be big, but the area boasted solid working farms, so businesses clung to life like barnacles to rock. However, this potential food-poisoning outbreak could work a financial tragedy on the community. He prayed that it didn't.

Ahead on his left, he spotted a blue, steel-sided building that sported a sign proclaiming Abbottsville Veterinary Clinic above a large picture window. The single-story clinic was barely the size of Kelly's modest bungalow, but much of her business would be going out to farms to treat livestock. Pets were probably the smallest part of her practice.

No lights showed through the window. It was too early for the front door to be open, so he wheeled his car to the back and found a pair of vehicles parked in a small area sheltered by pine trees. He parked beside Kelly's Explorer and got out. Shivering against a gust of bitter wind, he tromped toward a door set in a utility area that held a couple of kennels and a waste disposal site.

That was odd. The back door stood wide open. He couldn't picture meticulous Kelly being so careless. He stepped over the threshold and called her name. Barks and yips answered him. The hallway lay dark beyond the stretch of dawning daylight that filtered through the door behind him. He spotted a light switch on the wall and flipped it, then shut the door on the wintry blast invading the building.

A series of can lights in the ceiling spread illumination up the passageway. Matt's gaze froze on a form crumpled on the floor several yards ahead. His heart jumped.

"Kelly!" He charged forward and knelt beside her still body.

His neighbor looked as if she'd melted to the floor like an abandoned rag doll. The pale profile and blue lips were not a good sign. Matt touched the side of her delicate throat and then released a breath. Her pulse was strong and steady beneath his fingers. She moaned softly, and her eyelids fluttered, then popped open. A tiny shriek left her throat as she lunged into a half-sit, leaning on one arm.

"Take it easy." Matt reached out to steady her.

Kelly scrambled backward, avoiding his touch, her gaze wild.

"It's me. Matt. You're all right." At least he hoped that was true. "What happened?"

Her gaze found his and focused. The fear drained from her face. "I d-don't know…exactly." Her teeth chattered, and she hugged herself.

Matt scooted forward and wrapped his arms around her. She snuggled, her body shaking.

"Somebody g-grabbed me," she said. "And put something over my mouth, and everything went dark."

Heat burst through Matt's insides. Some lowlife had knocked Kelly out and then left the door open? If her attacker showed up this minute, Matt would show him cold, all right. In two seconds flat. Kelly buried her face in Matt's jacket, and he hugged her closer, willing his warmth into her.

"Tim!" The word burst out, garbled against the fabric of his jacket. She pulled her face away and stared up at him.

"You're saying some guy named Tim did this?"

"Of course not. Tim is my assistant. He was here ahead of me. His car is out back, but I haven't found him. We need to look. What if—" She pressed trembling fingers to her lips and struggled to rise.

Matt helped her up. "You're sure you're okay? We should call the police."

"Yes, and find Tim." She gazed around, dazed wildness again creeping over her face.

Whatever drug her attacker had used still had her disoriented.

"Listen." Matt took her arm. "Let's find you a place to sit down. We'll call the police, and then I'll look for Tim."

A low, human groan wafted from the area that housed the source of animal mewls and snuffles.

"The convalescent room." Kelly wobbled in that direction.

Matt caught up with her and supported her by the elbow as they entered a large area. A double row of cages filled one wall, half of them occupied by agitated pets.

"Tim!"

Matt followed Kelly's horrified stare toward the floor behind a worktable. Pet food was strewed across the linoleum, and a small bucket lay empty on its side. In the middle of the mess, a thin man sprawled on his back, unmoving. A red mask of blood covered his face.

Heart pounding, Kelly knelt by Tim's prone form and checked for a pulse. *Oh, please, God, let him be alive.* Air left her in a whoosh. *Yes!* A vein throbbed beneath her fingers. Tim groaned and stirred.

"Call emergency." She gazed up at Matt to see that he was already on his cell phone.

Tim moved, opened his eyes and tried to sit up. Kelly pushed him down. "Stay still. Help is on the way."

Seeing her assistant injured on the floor drove away the last vestiges of mental haze from the drug the intruder had used to subdue her. Her chilled body heated with a raw boil that flooded her veins.

Matt joined her at Tim's side. "What happened?"

Tim clasped a hand to his forehead, which sported a big goose egg and a bleeding gash. "D-dunno. Did I fall?"

"Not hardly." Matt spread his jacket over the injured man.

"Thank you." She ventured a smile at her neighbor. The guy was thoughtful. She should maybe thaw a little toward him. "The intruder must have hit you," she said to Tim.

"Intruder?" Her assistant puckered his brow and winced.

"Somebody attacked us and left the back door wide open."

"No wonder I'm so cold." Tim shuddered, then his brown eyes narrowed on Matt. "And *who* are you?"

"Hold your suspicions," Kelly said. "Matt's our rescuer. He's a state health inspector, and I left him at my sister's restaurant before I came here. The intruder was inside when I arrived. It's a good thing I'd invited Matt over to get those biological samples. We could have lain in the cold for who knows how long until somebody started looking for us."

Tim scowled, winced and then closed his eyes.

"This creep is pure meanness," Matt said. "I hope the cops catch him before he pulls another stunt like this."

She stared at her neighbor. The deep blue of his eyes had become as intense as an impending storm. He looked danger-ous...and attractive. She leaned back on her haunches, putting distance between them. Attraction was not an appropriate re-sponse at the moment.

Sharp raps sounded at the front door. Kelly surged to her feet, and the room whirled. A hand closed around her forearm, steadying her. She tugged away without looking at Matt and

headed for the reception area, well aware of his warm near-
ness following close behind. A black-and-white patrol car stood
outside the picture window, bubbles whirling.

"Thank goodness," Kelly breathed and opened the door to
Police Chief Art Strand.

The chief strode inside, a balding, sixtyish man of medium
stature with a middling paunch who'd been on the force in Abbottsville since Kelly was "knee-high to a grasshopper and
cute as a bug's ear." Or so he liked to tease her when they met
on the street. Right now, he was all business.

"You the one who called?" Art jerked a square chin at Matt.
He nodded and the chief turned his gaze on Kelly. "You all
right?"

"I am…or will be." She crossed her arms against a fresh
tremor. "Tim's hurt."

Art shook his head. "The fun never ends for that guy."

An ambulance pulled in beside the squad car, and a pair of
EMTs piled out. They all followed Kelly and Matt to where
Tim lay, pale and unmoving.

Kelly gripped Matt's arm. "He looks so…hurt."

The EMTs got busy with her assistant while Art's sharp,
gray gaze assessed the scene.

"The ambulance personnel are getting too much of a work-
out around here," the chief muttered.

"You mean, transporting people to the Sevierville hospital?" Matt said.

Art's eyes narrowed. "You know about that?"

"Matthew Bennett. I'm a state health inspector, assigned to
look into the case."

The chief pursed his lips and nodded. A pair of deputies
joined the melee in the room, which had suddenly grown too
small. Animal barks and yips and mews added to the chaos.

Kelly rubbed her temples where a headache had begun to
pulse. "I need to take care of my patients."

"Not until you're looked at by a medic." Matt awarded her
that intense, blue-eyed stare.

Kelly scowled. "I *am* a medic, and this is nothing that the passage of time won't fix. It takes a little while for the effects of improperly administered sevoflurane to wear off."

"That's what the guy knocked you out with?"

"I'd know that smell anywhere. He could have taken it from my pharmacy." Kelly sucked in a breath. She was an idiot for not figuring this out sooner. "The intruder was after drugs!"

She charged out of the room with Matt and Art on her heels. On the threshold of her pharmacy, she halted with a gasp. A tornado and a hurricane combined couldn't have trashed the place more thoroughly.

"Don't touch anything," Art's voice boomed.

Kelly's gut clenched. Matt settled a hand on her shoulder. Like a flower desperate for light, she leaned in to him. The grim reality of the last hour crashed over her, and her knees trembled. Someone had attacked her and Tim and had ransacked her clinic. Right here in Abbottsville. This stuff was only supposed to happen in the big cities.

"I need you to identify if anything's missing." Art jabbed a thick finger at Kelly. "Then I'll have to ask you to leave while I get a tech squad busy around here."

"But my patients." Kelly spread her hands. "Do your guys want to feed and clean up after a bunch of cats and dogs?"

Art scratched the thinning salt-and-pepper hair above his left ear. "All right. You stay. But only until everyone has picked up their pets."

Matt cleared his throat. "Would it be possible for me to take the package of biological samples Kelly collected from her patients yesterday? The samples may be pertinent to my investigation, and I can't imagine a burglar had any interest in animal waste."

"That's a fair bet." Art snorted. "Where was the package?"

"Here in the pharmacy." Kelly stared at the debris. Drawers had been ripped out of their frames and the contents dumped. Supplies had been swept from the shelving; the glass in the locked cabinet doors was shattered and the contents rifled.

Even the refrigerator door hung open with vials upended and tossed. "I don't see it."

Matt shrugged. "Not sure how you could spot anything in this mess."

Art held up a hand. "If my crew runs across it, they'll turn it in. One of my deputies will get with each of you and collect your statements."

Matt's brow furrowed. "I guess I'll move along then." His gaze fell to Kelly.

She squirmed on the inside. The warmth in the blue depths of his eyes was uncomfortably kind. This man was investigating her sister's restaurant. The last thing she should feel toward him was gratitude…or the desire to ask him to stay.

"Will you be all right?" he asked.

"Surrounded by most of the law enforcement in town?" She offered a casual smile.

"Still, be careful. I'll see you later, okay?"

She nodded. He'd see her later? A part of her did a happy dance. She squelched the sensation. He turned away and retreated toward a deputy who was holding a hand-size recorder. The officer beckoned him into the reception area.

She forced her attention back on the police chief. "After I tend the animals, can I use my office to call the pet owners?"

Art waved her off. "I'll send a deputy to find you."

Kelly made quick work of caring for her patients and then sought privacy in her office. The burglar had overlooked that cubicle in the corner of the building. She picked up the phone and started calling pet owners.

Getting them to come after their animals on a workday was easier said than done. A few offered to swing by over their lunch breaks. But Brenda had no way to collect her terrier until her second-shift cook came on mid-afternoon. Shortly, a deputy arrived at her office door. After giving her statement, Kelly settled behind her desk to stay out of law enforcement's way and catch up on paperwork…and miss Matt's reassuring presence.

How could she feel someone's absence so acutely when she'd only met the guy a couple of times? It wasn't merely because he was attractive. Looks were nice but pretty far down on her list of what made a good man. His reassuring air of competence, maybe? His integrity? So maybe his dog *had* trashed her Christmas decorations. Matt had taken full responsibility and collected the mess without a squawk. The way people were these days, common decency like that meant something.

Kelly shook her head to dispel the dangerous thoughts. The person she should focus on was Tim. Kelly called the hospital, and the receptionist rang her through to Tim's room. He greeted her in his characteristic glum tone.

"How are you doing?" Kelly asked.

"The doc put stitches in my forehead and says I have a mild concussion. They're going to keep me overnight in this holiday Hilton."

Kelly gave a dry chuckle. "Have you remembered anything about what happened?"

A pregnant silence answered, and then a sigh. "I'll keep racking my brains—whatever parts aren't scrambled. But the doctor says amnesia of events prior to a head blow is normal."

"I've heard that. I'm baffled about how the intruder got in. Did he follow you through the door when you unlocked it? Or did you know the person and let them in? Maybe—"

"I don't know!"

Tim's sharp distress halted Kelly's speculations. Gnawing on unanswerable questions was one of her worst faults. She annoyed even herself sometimes.

"You rest and get back on your feet," she said.

"Sorry, Kell. I didn't mean to snap at you. I'm pretty frazzled. Are you okay?"

"A little shook up but otherwise fine."

"That's a relief anyway. I couldn't stand it if anything bad happened to you."

Tim's concern warmed Kelly's heart. She hung up from the

conversation, biting her lip. Poor guy. He sounded alert but no more cheerful than his usual Eeyore self. Not that Kelly could fault his outlook too much.

In the past year, Tim had been through the wringer and then some. Frankly, there were a few necks she'd like to wring—his ex-wife, Hayley, at the top of the list, and a few mean-spirited community gossips a close second. It was a wonder he'd stuck around this burg the way every stitch of his dirty laundry, mostly nonsense, had been hung out to dry in public. While the divorce was pending and before Hayley skipped town, rumors had run the gauntlet of spousal abuse to infidelity. Hayley had milked the rumors for every ounce of sympathy, but Kelly hadn't believed a word of them. Not about the Tim she knew. The man had adored his wife. From Kelly's observation, Hayley had been the user and abuser in the relationship.

Hopefully, the assault at the clinic wouldn't prove the last straw for Tim and drive him from town. She'd heard about how insecure a home invasion made people feel. A business invasion was no better. Locking up, going home and hiding under the bedcovers sounded mighty appealing.

The desk phone rang, and Kelly jumped. She swallowed her heart back into place and picked up the receiver.

"Hi. It's Matt."

Like she hadn't recognized his voice on the first syllable? "Oh, hello. How's the investigation going?"

"Tedious." The word held more tension than boredom.

Kelly's stomach clenched. Had he discovered anything suspicious in regard to her sister's restaurant? She dismissed the ridiculous thought and brought her attention back to what Matt was saying.

"I was wondering how you're doing...and Tim, too," he said.

Kelly gave him an update and thanked him for the call. She could add considerate and thoughtful to Matt's list of virtues. Most guys wouldn't have given Tim—or her—a second thought. Smiling, Kelly returned to her paperwork.

When Brenda showed up after 3:00 p.m. to collect her dog,

she made a few sly comments about the good-looking, single health inspector, but Kelly dodged the remarks. What if she *was* feeling a flicker of interest in him? It was too soon to give her sister ammunition for a matchmaking quest—not that Brenda needed an invitation to embark on that project.

After her sister left, Kelly decided to call it a day. Tomorrow, she'd deal with her insurance company and clean up the mess. Snowflakes fell lightly on her shoulders as she locked the back door. A small shiver danced across her skin. Did some unknown party have a key for this lock? She'd call a locksmith, but who knew when one would come up to Abbottsville to install it?

The evening passed uneventfully except for her restless pacing around the lonely house. She couldn't concentrate on a movie or a book. Did the police have any leads on her clinic break-in? She parted her kitchen-window curtains. The house next door lay dark. She sighed. Her neighbor was disappointingly scarce. Had he gone out of town to turn in his samples? Was he interviewing the victims of the illness? She prayed he and his department solved the mystery soon so this dark cloud over her sister's business could disappear.

After a poor night's sleep disturbed by dreams of hands grabbing for her out of the dark, Kelly arrived walleyed and cranky at her clinic the next morning. Tim called around 10:00 a.m. to say he was being released from the hospital. A friend was giving him a ride back to Abbottsville, and he'd come to the clinic as soon as he could. She told him to go home and rest. With today being Friday, they wouldn't reopen until Monday.

A short time later, the insurance adjuster arrived and toured the building. The pharmaceuticals were the highest ticket items in the claim, but he agreed that the entire pharmacy inventory would have to be chalked up to a loss and destroyed, since they couldn't be assured that the intruder hadn't tampered with the medications.

After the adjuster left, Kelly started cleaning up. She saved the demolished pharmacy for last. Two hours of meticulous cataloging later, she was forced to a bizarre conclusion. Nothing was missing…except the biological samples intended for the lab. She called Art with her findings. If the police chief thought the theft of animal waste was as strange as she did, his cop demeanor didn't let on.

A few minutes later, she pulled up outside Brenda's Kitchen. Patrons were streaming out the door and standing in small, dumbstruck groups on the sidewalk. That was odd. Kelly climbed out of her vehicle and crossed the street. Closer, she spotted Matt with his back to her, facing the restaurant door. Art stood at his elbow, thumbs in his belt, looking way too official.

Kelly nudged her way through the crowd. She reached Matt as he turned away from the door. Their gazes clashed, then Kelly looked beyond him to the notice he'd posted on the door. Her nails chewed her palms.

"You're closing my sister's restaurant? No way! She's a clean freak. There can't be any contamination here."

Matt's brows pulled together above a frown. He took her elbow and guided her toward her Explorer. Kelly yielded for one purpose only—to hear what could possibly be said to justify this horrible action.

"Test results are conclusive." He halted in front of her vehicle. "It wasn't e. coli."

"Then what—"

"It was a concentrated dosage of phoratoxin, a poison found in mistletoe."

Kelly's jaw dropped open. This nightmare was no accident?

"Interviews with the victims—who have grown to eight, by the way—show one common denominator—Brenda's Kitchen. I'm sorry, but we have to close the restaurant to protect the public."

He looked genuinely mournful, but sorry wasn't going to salvage her sister's business. "Poison at my sister's restaurant? Impossible! The pets exhibited the same symptoms, and they never ate at Brenda's Kitchen. There has to be another explanation, and I'm going to find it."

Matt's mouth opened, but Kelly didn't wait for an argument. She hopped into her SUV and roared away, her appetite forgotten.

As each pet was presented for treatment yesterday, it was routine to ask if the animal had eaten anything out of the ordinary. The question had met with denials, but now she needed to push for better answers. Mistletoe? She pictured Matt's dog, Ben, gnawing on her wreath. But the Saint Bernard pup hadn't gotten sick.

Over the next hour, Kelly stopped at the houses of pet owners across town and probed to see if their animals could have ingested Christmas decorations. She was pulling all negatives in response. Dusk was falling, and so were her spirits. The initial flush of anger had long gone, and discouragement flowed in her veins. Festive Christmas lights adorned the homes she passed and mocked her with their merry twinkle. Hands in her jacket pockets, she walked past Chelsea's house, en route from one home to another in the same neighborhood.

A head-high chain-link fence surrounded the waitress's run-down, two-story residence. No Christmas decorations in evidence here. The only light filtered dimly through a back window.

Growls and snarls came from behind the fence, but Kelly paid no attention to Brutus, who paced parallel to her progress up the sidewalk. The Doberman probably remembered her as the evil human who poked needles into him yesterday. She was safe outside the fence, though. Too bad her quivering gut hadn't gotten that memo. If she'd had her brain in gear, she would have chosen another route to her destination.

Kelly reached the edge of the property, and Brutus threw himself against the fence. She jumped at the sudden rattle, heart leaping into her throat. Her pace quickened and took her across the deserted street. Impact against the fence sounded again, and then an ominous noise—the squeal of hinges. Kelly glanced over her shoulder as the dog surged through the gate.

Jaws wide, teeth bared, Brutus tore straight for her. Blood rushing in her ears, Kelly froze. This couldn't be happening.

Move, girl!

Her pulse spiked, and her feet grew wings as they flew up the sidewalk. She had one chance—the oak tree reigning over the yard dead ahead. Could she reach the safety of the cold, bare branches before dripping fangs closed on her flesh?

THREE

"The mistletoe poisoning has to be deliberate," Matt said to the police chief. They eyed each other across Art's office desk.

"Yep." The chief leaned back in his chair, gaze cop-flat.

"There's no way something that bizarre could be an accident."

"Nope."

Matt sat forward, elbows on knees, and ran the fingers of both hands through his hair. This case had gone from mishandling of food to attempted murder. And someone with access to the ingredients at Brenda's Kitchen had poisoned the patrons with malice aforethought. No wonder Kelly had reacted so angrily to the restaurant closing. A poisoner in her sister's restaurant? The thought scared him, too.

The phone on the chief's desk jangled, and Matt sat straight. Art answered, listened, scowled and then smirked. The man hung up and lifted a grizzled brow at Matt.

"Seems Kelly's been treed by a vicious dog."

Matt's throat tightened. "Is she all right?"

"She called in the report from her cell phone while perched on a branch. The dispatcher says she's fine, just cold and uncomfortable, because that dog won't let her out of the tree." Art rose and grabbed his hat. "Want to ride along?"

"Absolutely."

Matt followed the chief to a city-issue pickup truck with a

topper covering the box. Kelly might not be glad to see him, but he needed to see she was all right.

The short drive to a residential neighborhood passed in silence. They rounded a corner and came in sight of a gnarled oak in front of a house. A large dog prowled the base of the tree. The animal's snarls raised the hackles on the back of Matt's neck. His gaze found a slender figure standing on one branch and clinging to another higher up. As the squad car pulled over to the curb about a block away, the dog leaped toward the woman and nearly nabbed her heels.

Matt's fists clenched. "How are we going to lure that beast away from her without getting our own throats torn out?"

"No problem." Art sent him a sly grin. He grabbed one of the rifles in the rack behind their heads.

Matt's eyes widened. "Are you trying to get in trouble with the animal rights groups?"

"Tranquilizer gun." The chief winked. "In these mountains, we never know what kind of critter we'll have to take down and cart back to the wild. There's a cage under the topper."

He stepped out of the pickup, and Matt followed on nervous feet. The Abbottsville police chief better be a good shot.

"Am I glad to see you!" Kelly's voice wafted to them.

The Doberman answered with a spate of growls and a lunge against the tree. The animal didn't have a glance to spare the approaching men. Matt focused on the dog and stayed close to Art. The chief motioned them to a halt about two thirds of the way between the pickup and the tree. He lifted the rifle to his shoulder and narrowed his gaze across the sight.

"Don't hit Kelly." Matt's imagination toyed with a vision of her struck by a tranquilizer dart and tumbling from the tree into the dog's eager jaws. He shuddered.

Art sent him a disgusted look, then went back to perfecting his aim. Suddenly, the dog froze and stared in a direction across the street from them. Matt held his breath as the chief's finger tensed on the trigger.

"Don't shoot!" A stocky figure darted between them and the tree.

Art grunted and lowered the rifle. "Greg Milton. Brutus is their family pet. Some pet!"

"At least someone can nab the critter without you having to take a potshot."

Cursing in snarls almost as scary as his dog's, Greg grabbed the Doberman's collar and began dragging the animal across the street toward a high fence. Matt followed Art as they trotted toward the scene.

"Hold it right there," Art said to Greg.

The teenager threw the chief a hard look—half defiance, half fear. His knuckles were white around his dog's collar. The animal had ceased raging and now stood docilely, tongue lolling. If Matt didn't know better, he'd think Brutus oozed an air of pleased satisfaction.

Matt continued toward the tree where Kelly clung.

"Remember what I told you the last time Brutus took after someone?" The chief's voice followed him. "This dog is too dangerous to live in town. Put him in the truck. We'll have to notify the…"

The words were swept away on the wind as Matt approached the oak. Pale-faced, Kelly was trying to let herself down to a lower branch, but either a foot or a hand kept slipping. Matt reached the tree, and her grip slid again. She toppled forward. Matt reached up. Her slender figure hit him full force and knocked him flat backward onto the hard ground, forcing every ounce of oxygen from his chest. Their startled gazes met and locked. If her mouth opened any wider, she could swallow an egg. Air rushed into Matt's lungs, and he puffed out a chuckle.

Kelly's cheeks went from white to red. She rolled away and scrambled to her feet. "What are you doing here?"

"Hello to you, too." Matt rose.

She drew herself up stiff. "I owe you my thanks again."

His heart sank. He'd rather have her anger than her grudging gratitude.

Her attention left him for something beyond his shoulder. "Poor Greg." Her expression softened and saddened. "He loves that ornery dog. They're a matched pair of troubled souls."

Matt turned to see Greg race away from the police chief's truck. The kid tore through the opening in the fence, shut the clattering gate and disappeared through the side door of the ramshackle house. Art came around from the rear of the truck, where renewed snarls sounded, and headed toward the fence. Matt trotted across the street to meet him. He was as curious as the chief to investigate why the gate had come open. Kelly's footsteps pattered behind him. They met at the fence and stared down at the closed gate latch.

"What is that?" Kelly pointed toward a box built into the mechanism.

"They actually did what I said for once." Art snapped his fingers. "I told the Miltons they had to figure out a better locking system than a chain and padlock that they forgot to fasten half the time. This one's electronic. To open the gate, you have to punch in a code, but it locks automatically as soon as you shut it."

Kelly shook her head. "Someone must not have shut the gate firmly when they came through last."

"Negligence, any way you slice it." The chief scowled. "I've given Greg the lecture. I'd better have a talk with his dad. The kid says Nick's at home, but his mom's at the grocery store."

"Count me out." Kelly waved. "That guy gives me the creeps." She walked away.

Matt eyed Kelly going one direction and Art the opposite. He'd like to walk Kelly to her car, but she might think that was intrusive overprotectiveness. On the other hand, he'd love to meet this Nick character and gauge the guy's creep level for himself. Matt caught up with Art, and since the chief didn't order him to get lost, he considered himself invited for the interview.

They reached the sagging front stoop as the garage door rattled upward. A rust-bucket van roared backward down the driveway. Greg was at the wheel. The teenager seemed oblivious to their presence. He reached the street and gunned away.

Art sighed. "I'm going to end up arresting that kid someday. Just like his father. Nick's an ex-con who can't seem to stay on the right side of the jailhouse bars."

Repeated banging on the door drew no response. Art tried the doorknob, and it turned. Matt followed the chief into a dark, dank hallway. He inhaled and grimaced. The place smelled like air freshener striving feebly to mask the odor of dirty gym socks. From a room to the right, gurgling snores mingled with the blare of a television.

Art led the way around the corner. Matt halted beside him.

A brute with the build of a professional wrestler gone to seed lay sprawled on a ratty couch. He sported bristle on slab cheeks, one beefy arm cradled a mostly empty fifth of whiskey, and loud snores flapped a pair of blubber lips. Matt gave thanks that Kelly had opted not to join them on the expedition. The sight of this guy clad in a ripped and dirty undershirt and stained jeans was enough to ruin his appetite for a week.

"Wasted effort," Art growled. "I'll have to come back later."

Matt scanned the room. Someone had tried to make the place a little homey with knickknacks on shelves and pictures on the walls. Chelsea? It must be like nailing ice cream to a fence post to keep this place halfway clean while married to a slob. Round bottle stains marred the top of a cheap coffee table where a couple of remote-control boxes rested.

Without hesitation, Matt followed Art into the clean, cold air outdoors. They climbed into the pickup to a spate of growls from the crate in the rear.

Matt glanced toward the sound. "What's going to happen to Brutus?"

Art started the vehicle. "Someone from the Humane Society will evaluate the animal and determine if he's a candidate for a rehabilitation program. If so, he'll eventually be relocated with a fit owner."

"Sounds good to me. I wouldn't wish the conditions in that household on any animal, much less the people." Matt shook his head as snapshots of the ramshackle living room panned through his memory. His heart stalled as realization dawned. He slapped himself on the brow.

"What?" Art shot him a questioning look.

"Did you notice the brand names on those remote controls sitting on the coffee table?"

The chief pursed his lips. "Can't say I paid any attention."

"What was the brand name on the gate lock?"

Art's eyes narrowed. "Are you saying that the brand on one of the remotes matches the one on the gate lock?"

"You're no slouch in the deduction business."

"Apparently, I'm a slouch in the observation business." The chief struck the steering wheel with the heel of his palm.

"One of those two—Greg or Nick—could have seen Kelly coming up the street and opened that gate on purpose. It might not have been one of them carelessly neglecting to latch the gate."

"But there's no way on the planet to prove it either way."

"Nope." Matt's jaw steeled. "What motive would either of them have for turning their dog loose on Kelly?"

"Nick would do it for fun."

"But a person needs to be awake to push a button."

"That leaves Greg, and I have no idea why the kid would pull a stunt like that. He knew he'd lose the dog if there was another incident."

"What if he was the intruder at the clinic? A dead Kelly wouldn't be able to remember anything that would incriminate him. I saw the young man had a black eye."

"From his dad, most likely." Art shook his head. "Can't tell you how many times Family Services has tried to intervene in that household, but as soon as someone from the outside tries to come in, they clan up tighter than the Clampetts."

Matt cocked a brow at the police chief. "Maybe the shiner is from Kelly's elbow. She connected with her attacker."

Art frowned, then nodded. "It's a good theory. Leaves a few questions open…like why he broke into the clinic at all. There's nothing missing but that package of biological samples."

Matt opened his mouth, closed it and then shook his head. He needed to find a way to keep a close eye on Kelly. She'd suffered two attacks in as many days, and her business had been trashed. Now her sister's restaurant was under investigation for the poisoning of patrons. Could the real target of these activities be Kelly and her family? But why? If so, Kelly might not be safe anywhere.

"Brenda, we need to talk about this." Kelly spoke into the phone receiver while she paced around her living room. It was Sunday afternoon—two full days after the restaurant closing—and her sister still wouldn't open up about it.

"I can't, Kell," Brenda answered. "You know me. I need space to process shocks."

Kelly remembered—vividly—the days of silence from Brenda after their parents died. And again two and a half years later, shortly after Felice was born, when her sister learned she had breast cancer.

"The authorities will finish their investigation, and my staff and I will be cleared," Brenda said. "A few days at home will give me extra time to spend with Felice. I've been feeling neglectful of her lately."

"A few days—" Kelly bit off her words. If her sister wanted to live in denial that this could be the end of Brenda's Kitchen, she wasn't going to bust her bubble. Not now, anyway. "I'm here for you if you need anything. Two years my elder doesn't mean you have to be the strong big sister all the time."

Brenda's soft chuckle eased a measure of Kelly's tension. Since being treed by Brutus yesterday, she'd been jumpy as a bird at a cat convention, as their dad used to say. It was as if she was waiting for the next terrible thing to happen. But she wasn't about to lay her problems all on her sister. She hadn't bothered to mention the incident with the Miltons' dog.

"I know you're there for me, Kell," her sister said. "You always have been."

Memories of the long and frightening cancer battle passed through Kelly's mind. "Ditto, Bren." She had to trust they would emerge victorious from this trial, too.

Kelly's doorbell sounded, and a shiver ran down her back. What was the matter with her? She needed to get control of herself. Pronto.

"Guess I'll let you go," she said. "Someone's at my door."

"Maybe it's that cute neighbor of yours." Brenda giggled.

"Not funny. He's the guy who shut you down. Remember?"

"No, sister dear. Whoever put mistletoe in something I served at my restaurant is the one who shut me down. Matt was doing his job. Protecting people."

Kelly sighed. Brenda was right, but it was easier to be angry with big, solid Matt than a nameless, faceless crook. Besides, a strong dose of resentment immunized her heart against stirrings of interest she didn't want to feel.

The bell rang again.

"I'm coming!" She trotted to the hallway and flung open the door.

A generic greeting died on her lips as she stared into Matt's blue eyes and dangerously dimpled smile. Sunlight haloed his tall form.

"Hi," he said. "Do you feel like decorating?"

Kelly blinked. Her attention dropped to his arms, which cradled a stack of boxes labeled lights and garland.

A laugh parted her lips. "Did you buy out the store?"

"Pretty much." His grin—and the dimples—deepened. "How about it?"

"Let me get my jacket."

A minute later, she joined Matt in the yard where he was unpacking a string of lights. Ben barked a greeting and rose

to all fours from a sitting position. Matt pointed a finger at
the Saint Bernard and issued a command. The dog lowered its
haunches to the ground, tail wagging in the dusting of fresh
snow, which had fallen overnight.

"I'm impressed." Kelly laughed. "Have you been taking
him to obedience school?"

"Not yet." Matt handed her one end of the string of lights.
"But we're working on a few things at home. Maybe you can
recommend a school for him. For us, really. I need tips on
training him."

"You'd have to drive to Sevierville to participate in formal
schooling. Once you enroll, it's a strict commitment to attend
every class. With your type of work, that might be a challenge."

He grimaced. "I'm a dog owner. I need to man up to the
responsibility. Where do you want these?" He held up his end
of the lights.

"Around my door, I think. The nails to hook the wires are
already there. Ben couldn't dislodge those."

"Not for lack of trying." Matt chuckled.

They started fastening the lights while Ben played tag with
his shadow, carefree barks enlivening the air. Kelly smiled and
joined Matt in humming "Joy to the World."

"Maybe I could help you with the training at home," she
told him.

"Would you?"

"Sure." Kelly's face warmed. He stared at her like he was
thrilled to his socks. Why did she make the offer? She'd have
to spend more time with him and Ben. Well, the dog *was* adorable. She averted her gaze.

Okay, so was the owner.

They finished outlining the doorway with Christmas lights,
and Matt stepped back, surveying their handiwork. "What
next?"

"How about restoring order to the crèche?" Ben hadn't been

able to demolish the plastic figures, but he'd done a good job of scattering the scene.

The next hour passed in lighthearted banter and snatches of song as they replaced every strand and string of decoration that Ben had destroyed. All but the wreath. Kelly somberly contemplated the bare spot on her door.

"I got you a new one." Matt trotted up beside her.

He held out a fresh pine garland. "It's not mistletoe. I couldn't find one of those. I'm not happy that you lost an heir-loom because of my dog."

Her eyes unexpectedly misted. "That's okay. I'm not too fond of mistletoe right now." She hung the fresh-smelling pine boughs on the nail in her door panel. "It looks awesome."

"Thanks for being such a good sport."

Kelly studied the toes of her boots. "I was a brat. Could be baby sister syndrome…or a bad day." Or maybe because she found him too attractive and fought the feeling with everything in her, but she wasn't about to verbalize that option. She lifted her head and met his gentle gaze. No resentment on his face, just sympathy and understanding.

Ben scampered up and sat at Matt's feet, the animal's soft gaze a mirror image of its master's.

She lifted her hands in surrender. Who could resist those pairs of guileless eyes? "Come on in. Ben, too. Let me reward your generosity and hard work with a cup of hot cocoa."

Matt's lethal grin beamed down on her and sent her heart into gymnastic contortions.

"I can't think of anything I'd like better."

A short time later, they sat in opposite easy chairs in Kelly's small living room, cradling steaming mugs of cocoa topped with fluffy, white marshmallows. Ben sprawled on his side and fell asleep on the carpet between them. Puppy snores punctuated light conversation and laughter. Matt's gaze drifted here and there around the room. What was he looking for?

"Did you find it?" she asked.

"What?" He blinked at her.

"You keep looking around. Are you one of those white-glove-test guys?" She chuckled. "I confess. I haven't dusted in about a week. Not on my list of priorities."

"You caught me." Matt's face reddened. "I wasn't checking out your housekeeping. Just looking for the picture of the boyfriend that's got to be around somewhere?"

Kelly's insides tensed. "Why do you think I need a boyfriend?"

"I didn't say you *need* a boyfriend." He set his mug on a side table and clasped his hands together, elbows on knees. His gaze turned earnest. "The guys around here must be crazy if they're not trampling each other for an opportunity to get to know you better."

Her stomach went hollow, and butterflies flittered around the cavity. This must be what dismay and pleasure felt like at the same time. "I believe I've just been complimented, but I haven't been in the market for male companionship for a while. I got burned pretty badly almost one year ago to this day."

Matt's gaze dropped. "Aww. You don't owe me an explanation. I just—"

"It's okay. I don't mind." Strangely enough, she didn't at this moment. "My fiancé broke it off with me last Christmas. He preferred a high-society heiress to life in the sticks with a woman who wears jeans."

Matt sat up stiff, gaze darkening. "Some fool opted for country club and caviar when he could have had you?"

"Thank you."

"For what?"

"For calling Blake a fool."

"If the shoe fits."

Kelly sipped her cocoa, savoring the richness. Strangely, talking about her ex-fiancé wasn't turning her stomach to acid like it usually did.

"Up until my parents' deaths, Christmas was the happiest time of year for me," Kelly said. "I didn't lose my faith after the car accident that took their lives, but the excitement of the holiday vanished. Then my sister was diagnosed with breast cancer shortly after Felice was born, and I left school to provide support and look after the baby so her husband could keep working. That was another black Christmas." She grimaced. "Fortunately, Brenda survived, and I returned to school. When I met Blake, I dreamed of creating new family traditions. Then that idea blew up in my face with a Dear Jane letter in the mail a few days before Christmas last year." She let out a snicker. "I was feeling pretty sour this season. What your dog shredded were my hypocritical attempts at the holiday spirit."

"Blake sent a *letter* to break off an engagement? What kind of coward does that?"

Matt's scowl reminded Kelly of her father's when he saw hurt in, or a threat to, one of his daughters. The men didn't resemble each other physically, but they were both as protective as the day was long. Warmth filled her that had nothing to do with the cocoa.

"It had seemed so right." She laughed and set her mug on the side table. "We met at veterinary school in Memphis. Since we both came from small-town roots, we talked of returning to the simple life. Starry-eyed, I took him at face value. Then, boom! After I came back here to start a practice I expected him to join, Blake met a cute Memphis socialite. Her family connections offered him a taste of the high life, and he decided that a small town didn't have 'the proper scope for his talents.'" She bracketed the last phrase with finger quotation marks.

Matt snorted. "A heart of gold as pure as the tinsel on a tree."

"I hope he's happy with his choice." Kelly shrugged. "If that's what he wants out of life, we would have been miserable together."

"Good attitude. But you've been guarding your heart ever since." That intense blue gaze narrowed on her.

Kelly squirmed but met his look. "Guilty as charged. There isn't much of a field to play around here. A few farmers' sons.

But I've turned down every date I've been offered. It's more comfortable to socialize in groups instead of one-on-one."

"It's not a bad idea to start a relationship on a friendship basis rather than with romance. That's how Carrie and I first came to know each other."

Kelly's throat tensed. She should have known. Just because Matt wasn't wearing a ring didn't mean he wasn't in a relationship. She picked up her mug and studied the marshmallows melting in the pool of chocolate. Why should Matt's attachment status matter to her when she was determined not to be interested? Maybe Brenda wasn't the only one in denial.

She swallowed the silly lump that had formed in her windpipe. "What did Carrie think of your move to Abbottsville? Doesn't that place you in a long-distance relationship?"

A flicker of deep emotion passed over Matt's face. Pain?

"Carrie's in the best place possible but out of my reach." He studied his hands folded around his mug. "She passed away four years ago. Brain aneurysm. We'd been married twenty-three months and fourteen days. I'd just gotten off the phone from making reservations at an exclusive supper club for an anniversary surprise when I got the call…" His voice trailed away.

The air vacated Kelly's lungs. "I'm so sorry."

This man knew loss as deep as hers. Was he ready to move on? Was she?

His gaze lifted. "It's been a long haul. Relocating to Abbottsville is my starting-over statement."

Kelly's heart jumped. And Providence had placed him next door to her. Did that mean something? Her parents had taught her that God had a good plan for her life. Was Matt in it?

"Can I ask you a question?" he said.

"All right." Kelly held her breath.

Matt cleared his throat and shifted as if the chair had grown uncomfortable. "Is there any reason one of the Miltons would sic their dog on you on purpose?"

She exhaled. Whatever personal question she'd half expected, this wasn't even close.

He laughed. "You should see the look on your face. Sorry for blindsiding you, but that was a serious question."

Kelly envisioned Nick Milton's red-eyed glare over the counter of her reception area. Her scalp tingled. "There was no one in the yard when the dog escaped, though I have to admit that Nick likes me a little less than he dislikes most folks."

Matt chuckled at her wordplay, but Kelly grimaced. What she'd said was sadly true.

He opened his mouth, but his cell phone began to ring and he pulled it from a holder at his belt. "It's the office. I'd better answer." He listened to the person on the other end, lips thinning to a slash. "Right. I'll be on it in the morning." He holstered the phone with his gaze locked somewhere on the far wall.

"What's the matter?" A prickly sensation crept up Kelly's arms.

Matt heaved a long breath and met her stare. "An elderly victim has died of complications subsequent to the poisoning. His heart couldn't take the strain of the acute gastrointestinal distress. Evidently, he went into convulsions, and his heart gave out."

She gasped. "Who?"

"Bill Clemson. I assume you knew him?"

"Bill!" Kelly closed her eyes against a sweep of anguish. "Sweet old guy. Lived at Eunice and Amelia Simms's boarding house. A regular at Brenda's Kitchen." Kelly's eyelids popped open as a thought jolted through her. "Whoever put mistletoe in the food at my sister's restaurant is now a murderer!"

FOUR

Matt stepped into the Simms Sisters Boarding House early the next morning and stopped short just over the threshold. *Mistletoe everywhere!* No fewer than three doors led to the interior from the spacious foyer of the old Victorian house, and every ornately carved lintel sported a generous spray of the infamous plant.

"Come in!" gushed Amelia, the sixtyish-looking woman who met him at the door. Probably the same person he'd talked to on the phone to ask if he could drop by. "Our home is your home." Her words chirped like an often-repeated jingle.

She whisked his jacket from him, hung it on a wooden wall hook, and then bustled through the central door. Her old-fashioned floral housedress swished around her stout form. Matt trailed Amelia into a parlor decorated with vintage furnishings. The clean but faded area rug on the hardwood floor could be genuine, from early last century. But his attention was arrested by yet another spray of mistletoe hanging from a massive brass chandelier in the center of the room.

"Grandpapa had that piece shipped over from Italy when he built the house," his hostess said. "At one time it held candles. We've had it modified for electricity."

"Impressive," Matt said.

Amelia beamed. "How about a nice cup of coffee and a bowl of grits? Eunice is taking the pot from the stove."

Matt suppressed a wince. Until the poisoner was caught, he

wasn't eating a bite anywhere except at home—or Kelly's, if he had another opportunity. He sniffed the air. The place smelled more like apple pie than coffee and grits. The doorbell rang, saving him the necessity of formulating an answer.

Amelia rustled into the foyer, and Matt's ears perked up at a familiar voice. The woman returned with Kelly beside her.

Kelly's eyes widened. "You're here, too?"

"I might make the same observation." Matt grinned.

She colored. "I stopped to pay my respects on my way to the clinic."

Amelia repeated her invitation to share coffee and grits. Kelly declined, stating that she needed to get to work.

"I can't stay, either," Matt said. "The matter of your boarder's death is for the police to investigate. I only have a couple of questions for my report."

"Pooooor, dear Mr. Clemson!" The words came from an angular woman who rustled into the room bearing a tray of steaming cups and bowls. She set the tray on the coffee table and fanned her face with one hand. "It's hard to believe he's gone."

Amelia clucked. "But a mercy, though, I expect."

"A mercy?" Matt canted his head.

"His rheumatoid arthritis bothered him something awful." The sisters nodded to each other.

"He was in constant pain. Now he is at rest," Eunice added to her sister's analysis.

The doorbell rang again.

"Oh, dear," Amelia said. "We'll have to deal with a lot of company today." She didn't sound sorry.

Eunice answered the door and returned with the chief of police and a pair of uniformed officers. Amelia went white, then red, and wrapped plump hands together in front of her heart.

"Arthur, I knew you would come. Your timing is perfect. We were about to share a bite of delicious breakfast. Please, join us. I made it myself."

Eunice glared toward her sister, and Matt bit his lip against a chuckle. Kelly's gaze dropped toward her feet. She made no sound, but her shoulders quivered. The deputies exchanged grins behind their chief's back.

Art scowled. "No time for socializing. This is official business." He handed a piece of paper to Eunice. "This search warrant gives us the right to look for evidence of mistletoe extract on the premises. We will also examine the room where the deceased resided."

Eunice glanced at the sheet then sent her sister a broad smile. "How exciting, Amelia! We're suspects."

"I didn't say that." Art lifted his palms.

"You don't have to explain a thing, dear Arthur," Amelia said. "We've seen enough mystery shows on television. How can we cooperate? As you'll notice—" she waved an arm "—our establishment is adorned with an abundance of mistletoe. May I take you on a tour and show you all the places we've hung—"

"You may contribute nothing to the search whatsoever." Art's words were brisk. "It's too cold to make you wait outside, so you will have to stay in this room until we're finished."

The chief and his deputies dispersed toward different areas of the house. Amelia pouted her lower lip and plopped onto a claw-footed love seat covered in pink velvet.

Eunice perched beside her and patted her hand. "All is not lost. Arthur will smell the pies. You know what a sweet tooth he has. And you *did* make those."

"Pies?" Kelly spluttered a sound between a laugh and a gasp. "Why did you bake? Brenda's Kitchen won't need any today. The restaurant is closed indefinitely."

Matt looked from Kelly to the sisters. "You mean not all the baking is done on the restaurant premises?"

Kelly shot him a disgusted glance. "Lighten up, Mr. Government Employee. The Simms sisters' kitchen is licensed."

"Indeed it is," the women chimed in harmony.

Matt frowned. No wonder Art lost no time getting a search

warrant for this place. Not only did the dead man live here, creating an opportunity to develop motive, but his landladies could have had the means to do him in. Were the other poisonings a smoke screen for the real target? But what about the break-in at the vet clinic? The missing biological samples seemed to connect that crime to the poisoning. Who else but the culprit would have reason to steal the biological samples? Matt couldn't picture these two senior citizens clobbering Tim head-on or overpowering Kelly.

"I see those wheels turning." Kelly poked him in the arm.

Matt allowed himself a small grin. Lighten up, indeed. It wasn't his job to catch the crook, but to wrap up his report for his boss.

He turned toward the sisters. "Let me ask you a few questions, and then I'd better go."

"Me, too," Kelly said. "Go, I mean. Not ask questions."

Smiling, Matt pulled a small notebook and pen from his shirt pocket. "How long has Mr. Clemson resided here?"

"Eight years," Amelia piped up.

"No, sister, it's been at least nine."

"Eight. I remember distinctly. Mr. Clemson moved in the year the blight took our favorite apple tree."

"Yes, but that was nine years ago." Eunice's tone sharpened.

Matt cleared his throat. "So Mr. Clemson moved into your boarding house eight or nine years ago. What meals did he take here, and what meals did he eat out?"

"Breakfast here," Eunice said. "That's all we offer."

Amelia bobbed her chin. Matt hid an inner sigh of relief. No disagreement on that point.

"Then noon at Brenda's Kitchen," Eunice continued. "The restaurant is close by and has the only decent home cooking in town. In the evening, he generally heated soup on a hot plate in his room or made a sandwich."

"Except when you slipped him a serving of *our* supper," Amelia inserted.

"I never!" Eunice sprang to her feet and began dipping

spoonfuls of sugar from a server onto the cooling bowls of grits.

"Did too." Amelia glowered.

"Thank you, ladies," Matt said.

"We'll see ourselves out." Kelly touched his arm. Her green gaze danced.

Matt looked away before any chuckles could escape.

"You know who poisoned the food, don't you?" Eunice leaned toward them, gaze darting right and left as if a murderer lurked around the corner to overhear her.

"It was Chelsea." Amelia lifted double chins. "Had to be. Chelsea *serves* the food. That no-good son of hers gets his hands on the dishes *after* they've been used, and we would never suspect Brenda in a million years."

The sisters exchanged one of their nods.

"We could have been among her victims." Eunice continued where Amelia left off. "Every afternoon at precisely two o'clock, we go out for our daily constitutional and end up at Brenda's Kitchen for a glass of sweet tea and a slice of our own home-baked pie. What a stroke of Providence that we received unexpected company that day and didn't go for our walk."

"Quite right, sister dear." Amelia nodded.

"I'm late for work." Kelly's tone could have frosted a polar bear. "Share your theories with the police and no one else."

She marched toward the exit. Matt followed with the sisters close on his heels.

"Excellent advice," Amelia gushed. "I'm sure Arthur will be fascinated."

"And impressed that we've given the matter such thought," Eunice said. "You can even take the credit, if you'd like, sister dear. I know how much you want to attract the notice of our handsome police chief." The woman giggled.

Kelly flung open the door. Matt was amazed that a surge of cold air made it past the heat rolling off her. If her hair could burst into flames, it might. Leaving the sisters to their chatter, he followed Kelly up the sidewalk toward their vehicles parked at the curb.

"Are you all right?" He caught her elbow.

Emerald sparks snapped in her eyes. "The sisters' antics sometimes make me forget what gossips they can be. They fanned the flames across town when Tim was going through his divorce, and now they'll blacken Chelsea's name to everyone who will listen."

"How could anyone take them seriously?"

Kelly scowled. "Folks are looking for a scapegoat. Bill Clemson was well-liked."

"Sounds like the sisters feel his passing was for the best. You know what thought crossed my mind?" He flashed a grin. *"Arsenic and Old Lace."*

A hint of a smile formed on Kelly's lips. "The sisters did away with Bill as a mercy killing? If I was the gossipy kind, I'd spread that idea around. It might catch on." She looked at her watch. "Yikes! Tim is going to think I forgot to come to the office."

As they closed the distance to their vehicles, Matt studied her fine-featured profile and the gleam of her hair. Suddenly, Kelly halted with a cry and grasped his arm.

"Your tires! Who would do such a thing?"

Matt tore his attention away from her and looked at his car. The three tires within his view—both rear tires and the front passenger side—were pancake-flat. No need to wonder how. From the near hind tire, a knife hilt protruded.

Who would slash his tires? Matt's hands wound into fists. Try anyone among the fearful, angry public venting their frustration on the guy who'd closed Brenda's Kitchen.

Or the culprit could be a nervous killer sending him a message: *Back off or else!*

Tim's face wound into a scowl. "This town has gone insane. Poisoned pets and people, a break-in, someone dead and now slashed tires." He stood from the computer station behind the clinic reception desk and snatched a printout from the machine. "The craziness started when this Matt character moved to town. There's got to be a connection."

Kelly took the printout without glancing at tomorrow's appointment roster. They were about to close after another hectic day. Tim couldn't quit gnawing on the bizarre happenings in Abbottsville over the past week. She hadn't done much better at keeping her mind on work.

"Are you saying Matt slashed his own tires while standing beside me in the sisters' boarding house?"

Tim touched a pair of fingers to the patch of bandage on his forehead. "My brain isn't that discombobulated. I'm saying the timing has got to be more than coincidence."

Kelly laughed. "The guy came to our aid, and you don't like him."

"I don't like the way he looks at you." He sniffed.

Kelly's heart warmed. Eeyore her assistant might be, but he meant well. Over the past year, they'd commiserated with each other about their wounds in the relationship arena. Maybe it was time he allowed himself to move on. A fresh start at romance was becoming more attractive to her each time she encountered Matt.

"I'm not sure I mind the way he looks at me. It's nice to be admired." As Tim's mouth came open, she lifted a forestalling hand. "I'm not about to tumble off the deep end, but I'm willing to consider getting to know him. Life isn't over for you, either, you know."

"That's easy for you to say. You still have respect in the community. Everyone around here thinks I'm a mean-mouthed, cheating husband, and it's all lies!"

Kelly touched her assistant's shoulder. "Not everyone."

Moisture glistened in Tim's eyes. "I loved my wife. I would never have done anything to hurt her, but she wanted out so she encouraged the rumors."

"We've talked about this repeatedly, but I have to ask again. Have you forgiven her yet?"

"Some days, I think so. Some days, I still want to throttle her. But mostly—" his shoulders slumped "—I dream about getting her back. Then people wouldn't think I was such a loser."

Kelly suppressed a sigh. Not the best motivation for restoring a relationship. Besides, his ex had moved to Galveston, Texas, and was living with some guy she met online...while still a married woman. Tim could do better.

"I think God has the perfect plan for your life. He knows the truth. Lies don't stand with Him. Give Him a chance to make a difference to you, Tim."

Her assistant's brows drew together. Kelly held her breath. Was he listening this time or getting ready to blow her off again?

At last, he jerked the barest nod. "I suppose if I can't give my only friend's suggestion a chance, I'm a pretty sorry specimen." The corners of his lips nudged upward. "Tell me—"

The pop-pop of engine backfire claimed their attention. The Miltons' van rocked to a halt in front of the clinic's picture window, and Greg climbed out. His glare skewered them.

"Uh-oh!" Tim breathed. "Trouble on the hoof."

"I hope he doesn't think we have Brutus here."

The teenager stormed through the front door. "You did it on purpose, Kelly Granger."

"Did what?"

"Lured my dog outside the fence."

A laugh spurted between her lips, but she cut it off. The kid was serious. "Do you think I enjoyed being treed in the cold while your pet did his best to rip a chunk out of my hide?"

"My dad says you've been planning to get Brutus away from us for a long time. Maybe you saw the gate was unlatched and took your chance." Greg closed the distance between them. "Now I'm telling you to get him back."

"Just a red-hot minute!" Tim darted between her and the raging teenager.

The young man's fist shot out, and Kelly's scream melded with the smack of pummeled flesh. Tim went down, and Greg stepped over him on a course straight for her.

FIVE

Matt rammed through the veterinary clinic door. "Greg!"

His yell brought the Milton boy's head around as he reached for Kelly. Matt didn't wait to see what the kid would do next. He charged.

Greg turned, and Matt's shoulder connected with the teenager's midsection. They hit the floor. The kid's breath left him with a loud whoosh. Matt flipped him facedown, twisted an arm behind his back and perched on top with a knee on the kid's spine.

"Call Art," he directed Kelly.

She rushed past him and knelt on the floor beside her moaning assistant. The man sat up on one elbow, the other hand covering his lower face.

"Are you all right?" Kelly sounded breathless.

"I think by dose is broken."

"Your nose? Let me see."

He waved her away. "Call the police."

"Right." Kelly trotted behind the counter and grabbed the phone. She spoke briefly to the dispatcher, then turned back toward Tim. "Let me get some ice for your nose." She disappeared up the hallway.

A sob quivered the husky torso beneath Matt's knee. "I didn't mean nothin'. I just want my dog."

The kid squirmed, and Matt bore down with his weight.

"Your *nothin'* has left a man with a broken nose and scared a kind woman half out of her skin."

"Ow! You're hurting me."

"Then stay still. Maybe you haven't learned this lesson at home, but actions have consequences."

Greg heaved another sob. Long seconds ticked past, marked by Tim's nasal breathing.

"Good work, by the way," the assistant muttered. "But I could have handled it."

"Right. No problem." Their gazes locked, and Matt made a mental note. For some reason, this guy didn't like him.

Kelly whisked into the room, bearing a cloth wrapped around what Matt assumed was an ice pack. She bent over Tim and handed him the pack. The look on his face as he gazed up at Kelly answered the source of the animosity. Did she know her assistant was in love with her? Maybe she returned the affection. Matt's insides squeezed. For all the interest she'd shown in him, it was possible her heart was already claimed. Why did he hate that thought so much? They'd first met only last week.

Kelly came to stand over him and Greg with her fists on her hips, but her attention was on the teenager. "Your mom is going to be devastated. Isn't it about time you and your dad gave her a break from all this drama?"

The teenager didn't answer.

Matt met her frustrated look. "Are you okay? He didn't touch you, did he?"

"Thanks to your timely entrance, no. How did you get the situation under control so quickly?"

Matt shrugged and glanced away to hide his pleasure with her praise. Now he knew how his dog felt when someone patted him. "I was captain of the high school wrestling team. That was a long time ago, but I guess the skills never go away."

Wheeling lights strobed through the picture window, announcing the arrival of the police. Art and a deputy trooped inside. Matt gladly surrendered his charge to the deputy, who escorted a surly Greg to the squad car.

The chief cocked a brow at Matt. "Told you I'd end up arresting that kid some day. Didn't think it would be so soon. What happened?"

One by one, Kelly, Tim and Matt told their stories. Art listened and asked a few questions, then turned toward Tim, who now occupied a reception room chair. "Do you require transportation to the urgent care clinic?"

"I'll drive him over," Kelly answered.

"I'll ride along." Matt lifted a hand.

Above the ice pack, Tim's gaze shot daggers at Matt, but Kelly smiled. Art nodded and left.

"Isn't your car fixed yet?" she asked Matt. "I don't see it outside."

"The police had my vehicle quarantined where it sat for most of the day so they could collect evidence. Then it was taken to the garage. I was just over there checking on its status, but they weren't done changing the tires. Thought I'd kill a little time by dropping over here to say hello."

"I'm glad you did." Her look warmed Matt to the soles of his feet. If only he could discern if there was any personal interest fueling the gratitude.

Five minutes later, they pulled up outside Abbottsville Urgent Care. The town didn't have a hospital, but it did host a clinic to handle minor ailments and injuries. The waiting area was empty, so Tim was ushered immediately into an exam room.

Matt took a seat next to Kelly. "Looks like your assistant is developing a couple of shiners to go with the crooked nose."

Kelly heaved a sigh. "He took a punch for me…and a clobber on the head protecting the clinic. He may be a sad sack, but he's got guts."

"No argument there."

"What? About the glum attitude or the guts?"

"Neither." Matt grinned.

"Poor Tim." She shook her head. "Seems like everything bad happens to him."

Matt sat forward with his elbows on his knees. "I'm of the opinion that there's a spiritual law at work. Our attitude invites matching events. Not implying that Tim's to blame for Greg attacking him, or that bad things don't happen to happy people, too. Just a life principle."

"What you say is what you get." She nodded. "It's a choice to live under the circumstances or above them. Tim's been closed to any 'God-talk,' as he calls it, but our conversation was heading there when Greg burst in on us. I'm as angry with that young man for interrupting a priceless moment as I am about his crazy behavior."

Her gaze strayed to the hallway where Tim had disappeared. Thoughtful seconds ticked past. Matt studied the pattern in the tile floor. Did she wish she was in the exam room holding her assistant's hand? A green-eyed monster nibbled Matt's gut.

"What did you mean by asking me if any of the Miltons would have had reason to set their dog loose on me?"

"Huh?" He looked up to find her studying him. "Sorry. Woolgathering." He told her about the remote control. "Art said Nick would be a strong candidate out of sheer meanness, but he was passed out on the couch. If recent behavior says anything, Greg wouldn't be above pushing that button."

"I can't buy him risking custody of his dog. I even understand his fury today—not that it justifies his actions. People love their pets. Even mean ones."

"What if he's the one who broke into the clinic? Your elbow might have given him that black eye."

Kelly frowned. "I doubt my flailing struck anything with enough force to create a bruise. If equipment or drugs had been stolen, I could easily suspect a wild teenager. But to take a package of samples meant for the state lab when there was so much of material value? That's a huge stretch."

"What if the samples were taken because someone didn't

want proof positive that the rash of human illnesses and pet illnesses are connected?"

"I've considered that possibility, but the deduction doesn't point to anyone specific."

"So you're not going to consider Greg as a suspect?"

"It's the job of the police to consider suspects. To keep my sanity, I can't run around being paranoid of people I've known most of my life."

"Even when they punch out your assistant and go after you?"

"You win that point." She lifted her hands. "Maybe I should be a little paranoid of the Miltons—Nick and Greg, anyway. But I don't think either of them had anything to do with the poisoning or the break-in at the clinic."

He offered her a grin. "And how do you deduce that, Ms. Sherlock?"

"Elementary, my dear Watson." She poked a fingertip into his breastbone. "The poisoning was carried out by a shrewd mind. It wasn't a heat-of-the-moment impulse. Mistletoe extract isn't exactly available on the grocery store shelf. Nick and Greg are hotheads, not plotters. Besides which, statistically speaking, poison is a woman's weapon."

"Which brings us back to the Simms sisters."

"If they're eager to assassinate with their words, maybe they took matters a step further."

"I thought you weren't considering suspects."

Kelly's eyes widened. Her mouth opened but no sound came out.

"Never mind." Matt chuckled. "You wouldn't be human if you weren't trying to work this out in your head. We can only hope the police catch the culprit fast. Unfortunately, there doesn't seem to be much evidence to go on. We're still waiting for test results to pinpoint what food item at Brenda's Kitchen contained the poison. Maybe the local P.D. needs to call in help. I think Art's sharp and capable, but he didn't even take notes when we gave our statements at the clinic this afternoon."

Kelly snickered. "Arthur Strand has never forgotten anything in his lifetime, except his anniversary. He was in big trouble with Ethel every year until she died a while back."

"Making him the most eligible bachelor in Amelia Simms's eyes."

"Right. But I have a hard time believing she'd commit murder to get his attention."

Matt rubbed his lower lip between thumb and forefinger. "When this case is solved, we may all have a hard time wrapping our heads around the motive."

"Is that a prediction?"

"Call it a gut feeling. It takes a twisted mind to sabotage the food that a town full of people might eat—not to mention random strangers. Especially if the target was someone in particular. We don't even know that much for sure."

"In the meantime, my sister's business suffers, and she and all of her help are suspects."

Kelly's anguished gaze pierced Matt's heart. "I wish this character had struck through some sleazy dive, rather than a decent establishment. But I'm sure it's hurting restaurants all over town, knowing a poisoner is on the loose."

"Is that supposed to make me feel better?"

"Not really. The thought doesn't give me any comfort, either."

"Brenda doesn't hold hard feelings toward you." Kelly touched his arm, and the sensation reverberated to Matt's core. "Just wanted you to know." She withdrew her hand.

"Thanks." The word came out gruffly. "I'm glad about that. Do you have hard feelings?"

"I've been trying to nurture a few."

"Is it working?" Huskiness edged his tone.

"Not so well." Her words emerged a near whisper.

Their faces hovered inches apart. Should he close the distance? Matt felt himself falling into that soft, green gaze. Her generous lips parted. Matt eased nearer. She didn't pull away.

A throat cleared loudly. Kelly jumped, and her head swiveled. Matt looked up to find Tim frowning at them. A splotch of white bandage across the bridge of his nose matched the one on his forehead.

"Do you lovebirds mind taking me back to the office so I can get my car and go home?"

"Lovebirds?" Kelly rose with a too-high laugh. "We were deep in conversation. Come on. Matt needs to pick up his car before the garage closes." She looked at her watch. "We've got ten minutes."

She led the way to the door. Tim followed, leaving Matt to trail them. He scowled at the younger man's soldier-stiff back. Maybe he could find a reason for a detour that would make them late to collect his car. Then he'd have to ride home with Kelly. Maybe that would give him a chance to recreate his missed opportunity.

Or maybe, Mathew Bennett, the opportunity was all in your head.

If only he could see behind that lovely, inscrutable face to know what was in Kelly's heart.

Matt arrived home to an enthusiastic greeting from Ben. Too enthusiastic. He really needed to find the time to get into a dog-training program. Then his heart lifted, and he grinned to himself. What a pity he was so busy. That meant he'd have to take Kelly up on her offer to conduct the training.

His cell phone rang, ending his pleasant daydream of the two of them romping with his dog. He checked the caller ID screen but found no information.

"Hello?" His greeting was tentative. Some telemarketer had better not have found his cell phone number.

"Matt? It's Art."

He tensed. Not a telemarketer, but a call from the local police chief probably wasn't good. "What can I do for you?"

"Word has come down from the state, and our local police department is officially liaising with the health department on this mistletoe case. Your supervisor designated you the contact person."

"First I've heard of it, but I'm not surprised." A sour taste settled on Matt's tongue. Now that the source of the poison had proven to be something other than a food-borne pathogen, he'd hoped to distance himself from the investigation that threatened Kelly's sister. No such luck.

"I'm calling to inform you that I'm getting a search warrant for Brenda Tanner's residence. We go in tomorrow."

"Do you require my presence?"

"Negative, but we'll keep you informed."

Matt let out a breath. Thank goodness for small favors. At least he wouldn't have to admit to Kelly that he'd taken part in a search of her sister's home. Matt closed the call, praying that nothing incriminating would be found at the Tanner residence.

Kelly studied the display of apples at the grocery store as if the fate of the world rested on her choice of fruit. Had she really almost let Matt kiss her yesterday afternoon?

Last evening, while she shared a meal and a movie with a quiet Brenda and an active Felice, she'd asked herself that question about the kiss-that-never-was. Good thing she hadn't let on to her sister that her attraction to Matt was growing faster than she would ever have thought possible. She'd never hear the end of it. Today at the clinic, visions of his strong face and deep blue eyes had done their best to distract her.

It had been another difficult day with a farm emergency on top of the regular appointments. Tim had come in more depressed than usual. There had been no way to turn the conversation back to spiritual things. In fact, she'd let him go home early. The puckers between his brows had betrayed a headache. Now, she wanted only to pick up some fruit and sandwich fixings and head for home.

She plopped a pair of apples into a plastic bag then turned and almost barreled into Amelia Simms.

"How lovely to see you." Amelia fingered her dress's lace collar. "I'm sure you've been wondering what the police found at our house?" The woman leaned close. "Nothing but rat poison!" Her stage whisper drew more attention from passing shoppers than a normal tone would have.

Kelly's face heated. "I doubted they'd find any—"

"I suppose it was only natural that the authorities would move on to another logical suspect." Eunice glided to her sister's side. "Though if you ask me, they should have searched *her* house first."

"Whose?" Kelly looked from one woman to the other.

The sisters shared a glance.

"You don't know?" Amelia sounded shocked. "We assumed she would call you."

Eunice nodded. "We wouldn't know ourselves except we drove past the house and saw the squad car at the curb."

Amelia grabbed her sister's arm. "You don't suppose she's been arrested, do you?"

Their meaning dawned on Kelly. *Brenda!* She tossed her apples onto the display and headed for the exit.

"If she were in jail, sister dear—" Eunice's voice trailed her "—she would at least get one phone call."

Minutes later, Kelly pulled up in front of Brenda's rambler house. Lack of a squad car out front brought no comfort. She hammered on the door. No response. Kelly tried the latch. It was open, and she stepped into a darkened foyer. The piney fragrance of a holiday reed diffuser greeted her. A muted sob drew her feet toward the living room. No lamp brightened the gloom of dusk in that room either—not even a glimmer from the Christmas tree standing dark sentry in the corner. But she made out a figure hunched over on the couch.

"Brenda!"

The sniffles cut off, and her sister's face lifted. "Kell?"

"What's going on?" Kelly knelt in front of her sister. "I heard the police were here."

Brenda wiped her nose with a tissue crumpled in her hand. "They were."

"Did they accuse you of something?"

"Not in so many words, but I'm surprised Art Strand didn't arrest me on the spot."

"Why? There would need to be strong proof."

Brenda flopped against the back of the couch. Kelly had never seen her sister's face so hopeless. A chill encased her heart.

"They asked me who makes the sweet tea," Brenda said. "I had to admit that I personally make it each day."

"So the poison was in the tea?" Kelly stood up. "Anyone with access could have put something into it when your back was turned."

"Which leaves few suspects. I don't let just anybody traipse through my kitchen."

"Then I'm a suspect, too. I drop in on a regular basis."

"Yes, but you never had breast cancer."

"What does that have to do with poison in the tea?" Kelly's brow puckered.

Brenda sat up and ran her fingers through disheveled hair. "I need to get Felice from the babysitter's house. I dropped her off there while the police searched the place."

She started to rise, but Kelly pressed her down on the couch and perched on the edge of the coffee table. "You're not moving until you tell me what the police found."

"It's what they didn't find." The last word came out a wail.

Kelly had no clue what her sister meant, but she moved onto the couch and wrapped Brenda close, absorbing a fresh spate of tears. The storm finally receded, and Brenda eased away.

"You must think I've lost every marble in my head." She dabbed at her face with the tissue.

"The thought crossed my mind."

Brenda offered a weak smile.

"What *didn't* the police find that's got you upset?"

"Do you remember when I was in the midst of chemo treatments, and things didn't look good?"

"I'll never forget."

"Nobody thought I should try the experimental drugs I researched on the internet."

"The effects were unproven and unpredictable."

"I know." Brenda nodded. "Turned out you were right to trust God and the doctors, but I—" Her gaze fell, and she picked at imaginary lint on her slacks. "I got a homeopathic doctor to prescribe Iscador for me anyway. I chose the oral kind, because I didn't want injections. I was getting enough of those."

Kelly's brow puckered. "Iscador? Was that the herbal treatment?"

"Yes. Do you remember the main ingredient?"

Kelly searched her memory and then gasped. "Mistletoe!"

Back when they were fighting for her sister's life, Kelly had researched Iscador as soon as Brenda mentioned it as a possible treatment. But the theory behind its use to fight cancer was somewhat speculative and mystical, though its proponents claimed the drug boosted the immune system, mitigated pain and slowed the growth of cancer cells. The drug was used primarily in Europe and very little in the U.S., due to lack of solid, clinical evidence for its benefits. Kelly had strongly discouraged Brenda from trying an unproven treatment that involved a poisonous herb, but Brenda had been desperate, and Kelly didn't blame her for that.

She squeezed one of her sister's hands. "You wanted to try anything possible to survive and raise your child. I get it."

Brenda's head lifted. Her face was grim and composed, more like the tough big sister Kelly knew best. "Your reservations about it bothered me, so I couldn't bring myself to take the drug, and shortly after I got the shipment all the way from Europe, I was pronounced to be in remission. The container has been sitting in my bathroom closet ever since."

"Did you tell the police about the Iscador?"

Brenda shook her head. "I didn't remember it until after they'd left. Then I looked, and the bottle was gone. No wonder the authorities didn't find it."

"Gone? Someone took it? When? How?"

"Your guess is as good as mine." Brenda spread her hands. "It's going to look bad for me, but I have to tell the police about the missing Iscador."

Kelly bit her lip against a protest. "A part of me wants to beg you to keep your secret."

"Then someone will get away with murder."

"I know." She sighed. "Our parents would roll over in their graves if we weren't honest. I'd like to go with you when you report the theft."

"I'll make a sweep through the house tonight to make sure it didn't get mislaid. If I don't find it, I'll go see Art tomorrow."

"Call me, and I'll be right at your side. How much of that stuff did you have?"

"Several ounces. The instructions mandated a small dosage at first, increasing gradually over time and tolerance. But it doesn't take a rocket scientist to figure out that if the whole bottle were dumped into tea, there was more than enough to make many people very sick." Brenda visibly shuddered.

Kelly snorted. "Any type of treatment for cancer is poisonous, even herbal treatments. I did some homework after mistletoe was identified as the poisonous agent that made the pets and people ill. Mistletoe can cause nausea, vomiting, diarrhea, blurred vision, raised blood pressure, the collapse of blood vessels, convulsions—"

"I know. I know," Brenda interrupted. "That's why the dose has to be carefully regulated. Just like with chemo and radiation. The treatment carries risks."

"Tell me about it." No one would know it to look at her now, but Brenda had sometimes been at death's door from the chemotherapy. There was no way Kelly was going to lose her now to a cold prison cell. "We have to figure out who took the Iscador."

"What? You're going to interview everyone who's visited since my bout with cancer? Less than two weeks ago, most of the town came through for my Christmas open house."

Kelly swallowed a groan. Brenda tried new recipes for the restaurant at her annual Christmas party. People attended in droves.

"What about Nick?" she blurted.

"Nick Milton?"

"He created a horrible scene at your party—and you weren't serving any alcohol. Art had to throw him out."

Brenda scowled. "I never did figure out why he ranted at a room full of guests that we were all against him and his family. Poor Chelsea would have slunk out with her head hanging low if my staff and I hadn't rallied around her. Why? Do you think Nick could have taken the Iscador?"

Kelly frowned. "He doesn't seem bright enough to plan such an elaborate revenge. Besides, how would he know what Iscador is or what it could do?"

Sharp whines came from the rear of the house.

"That's Bo." Brenda rose. "I shut him in the garage while the police were here." She clicked on a table lamp, and Kelly's heart twisted at her sister's splotchy face and red eyes.

"He probably needs to go outside." Brenda led the way to the kitchen and opened the doorway into the garage.

A small bundle of dark, curly fur yipped and scampered inside, stub tail a blur of waggles. Kelly scooped the terrier up and received enthusiastic kisses on her chin. "You go get Felice. I'll look after Mr. Bo Jangles."

Brenda hugged her. "You tease me about being the strong big sister, but you've been a rock for me more times than I can count."

Kelly forced her lips to curve upward. "We'll get through this, too."

It wouldn't do to let her sister see that fear wrapped her

heart. The poison was administered to people at Brenda's Kitchen through tea made by Brenda with drugs bought by Brenda. How much more evidence would the authorities need to make an arrest?

SIX

Matt pulled up outside the veterinary clinic. The morning sun offered a good view through the picture window. He glimpsed the top of Tim's head bent over the reception desk. Kelly must be in the back, looking after patients. As much as he didn't want to interrupt her business, with all the strange and dangerous events that had been swirling around her, he'd feel neglectful if he didn't remind her he was available if she needed anything.

He got out of his car and headed for the front door as a woman exited, cooing in a yellow cat's ear. Matt sidestepped as she swept past him, oblivious to his presence. Shaking his head and chuckling, he entered the clinic. While he was dodging the cat owner, Kelly must have emerged from the exam area. She stood beside Tim at the counter.

They looked up as he came through the door. The assistant's face was a montage of greens and yellows, overlaid by strips of white bandage, but his gaze was bland. Kelly's was edged with frost, and she turned her head away. *Uh-oh!* She probably associated him with the search at her sister's house, whether he'd been there or not.

"How are you doing?" Matt said to Tim.

The question elicited a glance and a small smile from Kelly. She liked him being nice to her assistant. Did that bode well for his interest in her, or was it a sign of favor toward Tim?

"Healing," Tim said and went back to his work at the desk.

Kelly tucked a stray strand of red hair into the professional chignon at the back of her head. "What are you up to today? I thought you'd be out chasing down careless restaurateurs."

The statement held no sarcasm, so Matt took it at face value and smiled. "I'm catching up on paperwork at home." His smile faded. "I heard about the search at Brenda's house. At least they didn't find anything."

"Right." Kelly's gaze darkened, and she looked down at some papers on the desk.

What had he said to set her off? He cast around for another topic. "I talked to Art this morning, and I thought you might like to know that the knife in my tire was wiped clean of fingerprints."

"No suspects then?" He had her attention again.

"Not yet. They didn't find any witnesses in the neighborhood, either."

Tim handed Kelly a file folder. "Most folks are at work that time of day, so I'm not surprised. And less surprised that this hoodlum got away with slashing your tires right under the noses of our able police department."

Kelly shot a frown at her assistant, then sent Matt a long-suffering look. He stifled a grin. Eeyore, all right.

"Have the police been investigating the pet poisoning?" she asked. "I still believe that angle might lead to the culprit who tainted the tea at Brenda's Kitchen."

"They've interviewed the same pet owners you did, but got no better results."

Kelly's cheeks went pink. "A day of infamy I'd rather forget."

"It's criminal!" Tim shot from his seat. Red turned his face into a full set of Christmas colors. "Excuse me, but I get riled every time I think of anyone feeding poison to defenseless animals." He stalked from the room.

Kelly's gaze followed him and then turned toward Matt, brow puckered. "Tim is sensitive about the patients we serve, which makes him a great veterinary assistant."

"He seems to care more about animals than people."

"He's had a lot of disappointments with people." She shook her head. "He hasn't figured out yet how to find the good in spite of the bad."

"If anyone can help him with that, you can."

Kelly beamed.

Finally, he'd said the right thing—except it had been like an open suggestion for her to spend more time with her assistant. He could pat himself on the back and kick himself at the same time. The mental picture put a goofy grin on his face, which she mirrored. The silent meeting of the eyes held for long, sweet seconds, then her gaze suddenly shuttered, and she looked down at the file in her hands.

Matt cleared his throat. "I just wanted to let you know I'm around if you need anything."

"I appreciate the thought," she said, though her attention remained on the file.

"I'd better let you get back to your paper shuffling, while I return to mine."

"Sure. Thanks for coming in." Her weak smile was dismissive.

Matt walked to his car with his heart dragging behind him. It had taken him months to fall in love with Carrie, but Kelly had snagged him when those gorgeous emerald eyes snapped at him during the first scold over his decoration-ravaging dog.

He drove home and stopped by the mailbox at the end of his driveway. He powered down his window and retrieved his mail. Among regular, white envelopes and an outdoorsman's catalog, a brown manila envelope without address or postage caught his eye. Whatever the packet contained was thicker than a magazine, but soft and squishy. Not a bomb then. He chuckled at his mental drama even as he eyed the clip that held the flap shut. Whoever put the envelope into his box wasn't the mail carrier and hadn't sealed it. He didn't have X-ray vision, so opening the envelope was the only way he was going to find out what was inside.

Should he take it to Art first? He'd look like an idiot if it was a solicitation from some local kid to support their fundraiser. Matt set the mail aside and pulled his car into his driveway. Then he grabbed the mystery packet and opened it.

Hair! Wads of it. And of a color he recognized.

Matt threw the packet aside and leaped out of his vehicle. He raced into the garage where he'd rigged an indoor pen with outdoor access for his dog while he was away. Ben wasn't inside. Matt called, a frantic edge to his voice.

No response.

Pulse jackhammering, Matt called again.

A familiar *whoof!* answered. Then the Saint Bernard burst through the hinged flap between the indoor and out-door pens. The animal rose on his hind paws and hit the fence with his front paws amidst his usual enthusiasm of barks and tail-wagging.

Breathing thanks to God, Matt opened the gate and wrapped his arms around his pet's neck. Ben anointed every available inch of his master's skin with his tongue, and Matt didn't pro-test. He ran his hands through Ben's fur, then stopped cold when he met stubble. Matt held his dog away from him and studied the animal's left side.

His marrow turned to frost.

While he'd been gone, someone had come to his house and shaved a bull's-eye in his dog's fur.

Something rotten in this burg was about to bust wide open. Kelly sensed it lurking so close, her scalp prickled as if some-one had breathed on her neck. Maybe she was catching Matt's "gut feeling."

When he stood in her clinic this morning, exuding compe-tence and caring, she'd battled an impulse to blurt out her sis-ter's secret and ask his advice. But the missing Iscador wasn't her information to share. When Brenda called to say she was ready to go to the police, Kelly would suggest enlisting Matt for moral support. How far she'd come from feeling like he was a threat! Not that Matt's sympathy would keep Art from doing his duty and arresting Brenda, but if Brenda got led away to a cell, Kelly would need arms to collapse into, and she wasn't too proud to pretend otherwise.

She glared at the silent phone on her office desk. Why hadn't her sister called? Had she decided not to inform the police about the Iscador? Wicked hope leapt within Kelly. If she had to choose between keeping her sister out of jail and letting a killer escape man's justice, she'd pick her sister. God forgive her!

The phone rang, and she jumped as if she'd been sitting on a spring.

"Hello?"

"Hi, sis." Brenda's dull tone knotted Kelly's stomach. "I told Art what his search squad *hadn't* found."

"Why did you go without me?" Her spine went rigid. "You're not calling from jail!"

Brenda let out a limp chuckle. "No, I'm not wearing an orange jumpsuit, Miss Mary Sunshine…not yet, anyway. You've been so swamped at work, I didn't want to disrupt your day with my errand."

"What happened?" Kelly planted her elbows on the desk.

"Art said the state lab would test for ingredients specific to Iscador. If the tests came back positive, then…well, you know how police are. He said something noncommittal, but he followed it with that ominous warning about not leaving town."

Kelly's heart dropped into her toes. "So you continue in a limbo of impending arrest."

"More time with Felice, I guess."

"You hang tough, big sis. Maybe the poisonous mistletoe will turn out not to be from Iscador after all, and then we're home free."

"Except a killer remains on the loose, and my restaurant is still closed."

"Okay, not out of the woods totally. But we will be. I promise!"

"You'll thank me that I don't plan to hold you to that promise."

They chatted briefly about other things, like Felice's latest accomplishment of saying her full ABCs, then ended the call. Kelly cradled the phone, resolve forming. She wasn't going to wait for test results that threatened her last shred of family. If the police couldn't shake any evidence loose, maybe someone who didn't wear an intimidating uniform could tempt information from the one person, other than Brenda, who was most likely to have glimpsed unusual activity at the restaurant. Chelsea might not realize she'd seen something important. A little woman-to-woman chat between a pair of people who loved Brenda might be the grease needed to gain new insights.

She got on the phone to the Milton residence. Chelsea answered on the first ring. The tenor of her greeting betrayed this was a day the woman was being quiet around the house to keep from annoying her hungover husband.

"Want to get out for some fresh air?" Kelly infused cheer into her tone. "I'll bring coffee from the convenience store, and we can enjoy the sunshine on a walk around the neighborhood."

"Make mine cocoa, and you're on." The woman sounded pleased. "But park out of sight. I don't want Nick to know I'm meeting you. He's not too happy with your family right now. I'll watch for you."

Kelly stripped off her lab coat and grabbed her jacket. She stopped in the convalescent room and looked in on Tim, who was cleaning the vacated cage of a recently spayed feline. Two other animals, not yet ready to go home, lifted their heads and gazed at her.

"I'm going to be out for an hour or so," she told her assistant.

He rounded on her. "You're up to something."

"Nothing earth-shattering. I'm going for a walk with Chelsea."

Tim frowned. "You're nuts to put yourself within ten feet of anyone in the Milton family. I don't like it."

"Chelsea? C'mon! I'll stay away from Nick, and Greg is in jail." A place she was determined her sister would never see.

Tim's glower followed her out of the building. Fifteen minutes later, she parked her car a block down the street from the Miltons, and spotted Chelsea watching for her from the corner of their yard. The older woman waved and tromped up the sidewalk. A bright day and mid-forties temperatures had dried the cement from recent snowfall, except for small, damp areas that steamed under the sunshine. Kelly handed Chelsea the insulated cup of cocoa, and they fell into step on a course away from the Milton house.

"I'm glad you called," Chelsea gushed. "I'm so upset about Greg, and I needed to talk to someone. Who better than the person who can put in a good word for him with the judge? You will, won't you?"

The woman stopped and gripped Kelly's arm. The waitress's dark eyes pleaded with her. Kelly opened her mouth, but an appropriate answer wouldn't come. What had she expected? Kelly's priority might be Brenda, but Chelsea's concern would naturally be her son.

Kelly took a deep breath. "Tim's looking the worse for wear. Greg frightened me, but he didn't hurt me. He could have, though."

"I know." Chelsea dug a fist into the pocket of her well-worn coat. "I've tried to raise that boy right, but he's got his father's temper, and he loved that dog." She led the way up the sidewalk. "Can't say I cared much for the dirty thing, but Greg thought the wiggle of its tail stub hung the moon."

"Believe me, I understand the attachment people have for their pets."

"I figured you would." A smile darted across the woman's face. "That's why I hoped you might drop the charges. It's a lot to ask, but I don't want my boy saddled with a record like his daddy. Nick has applied all over town, but no one will hire him because he's an ex-con."

Kelly bit her lip. The man's lack of work wasn't the fault of his past as much as his present behavior. Evidently, Chelsea didn't see it that way.

"I know everybody thinks he's a worthless drunk." The waitress kicked a stone off the sidewalk. "Those Simms sisters had the gall to say out loud to guests at Brenda's Christmas party that we Miltons are trash."

Kelly's jaw dropped. "You heard them say such a thing?"

"I didn't, but Nick did. That's what set him off. A guy can't let folks talk that way about his family. Then he's the one who got kicked out of the party, not those mean old biddies." Chelsea's eyes shot sparks. "Someone ought to give them a taste of their own medicine."

Kelly's mouth went dry. Maybe someone had tried. Chelsea looked hot enough to be the hand of retribution. Kelly would never have guessed the long-suffering head waitress at Brenda's Kitchen had so much fire in her. Maybe the Simms sisters were the target of the poison, but because of their unexpected company that day, they never showed up at Brenda's Kitchen to indulge in their treat of sweet tea and slices of pie.

"What did you say?" Kelly shook herself.

"I said, Nick used to be the sweetest guy. Then stuff happened to sour him. When Greg was little, and we lived in California, we ran into some bad money problems. Nick did things he shouldn't have done, in order to make a fast buck, and got caught. He did his time. Me, too." She stared up at Kelly. "Five long years, I raised our boy alone. Then he came home, and we moved to Abbottsville, where Nick grew up. He figured folks he knew would give him a break. I thought things would get better, too, but a con's past follows him around." The woman dropped her gaze toward the cement passing beneath their feet.

Kelly refrained from reminding Chelsea of all the time Nick had spent cooling off in the county jail over a drunk and disorderly charge or a domestic disturbance. She knew a fellow who worked over at the feed store and had a criminal record for some pretty rough stuff, but he'd straightened out after his release and was a valued employee, a decent family man and accepted in the community.

"It must be hard with the restaurant closed, and no one bringing home a paycheck," Kelly said as they rounded the corner onto another block.

"Tell me about it." Chelsea rolled her eyes. "Nothing to do, nowhere to go and no money to do nothing with." She let out a brief chuckle at her play on words.

Kelly laughed with her. At least circumstances hadn't annihilated the woman's sense of humor. "It's in everyone's best interest to catch whoever slipped the mistletoe into the tea."

"Yeah, I heard the rumor that the poison was discovered in the sweet tea."

"Did you notice anyone in the kitchen who didn't belong? Or maybe someone who belonged but was acting unusual?"

The waitress squinted toward the white-capped mountain humps on the horizon. "Honestly? I can't recall a thing out of the ordinary during my shift on the day people started getting ill. Brenda's particular about who she lets into her kitchen. Of course, the sweet tea is kept in a refrigerator behind the server's counter. But that's out in the open, and it would be almost impossible to slip something into the pitcher in full view of every patron in the place."

Kelly frowned. Unfortunately, Chelsea's words pointed strongly to the poison being mixed into the tea during its preparation—before it was placed into the public eye for serving. Brenda prepared the sweet tea every morning, which limited the possibilities to personnel on duty early in the day. Greg did dishes before and after school, which gave him opportunity. But she had a hard time picturing the volatile teenager as sly and calculating. He could sling a fist in the heat of the moment, but plot and plan and slip the town a lethal Mickey? The act seemed out of character. Hadn't she said poison was a woman's weapon?

Kelly shot a sidelong look at her companion. The woman's expression seemed puzzled but open. Had the waitress missed her calling as an actress? Maybe Kelly was trying to pry information from the person who knew exactly what had happened. Chelsea's anger with the Simms sisters gave her motive, and she would have had opportunity to steal the Iscador from Brenda. As a friend, as well as her employer, Brenda often welcomed Chelsea into her home. She would probably be aware of the nature of Iscador, because Brenda would have discussed her treatment options with Chelsea. The logic made horrible sense. Cold fingers danced down Kelly's spine. Had the Simms sisters guessed right? Could she be on a stroll with a murderer?

"Maybe we should head back toward your house," she suggested.

"Fine by me. I'm done with this cocoa, anyway." The waitress tucked the empty cup into one of her coat pockets. "About Greg, I know you'll decide the right thing. You and Brenda are the salt of the earth. Can't say I'm so sure about Tim, but you've got pull with him. I'll make my boy get on his knees and apologize, if it'll help get those charges dropped."

"I'd like to talk to Greg about the things I've discussed with you. Maybe I'll stop by the jail and visit him."

Chelsea eyed her soberly. "You might not like this, but I need to tell you about Greg."

"That's a bull's-eye, all right."

Art frowned down at Ben while Matt held the squirming pup for inspection. They stood near the Saint Bernard's outdoor pen behind the garage. Ben was about jumping out of his skin trying to make sniffing acquaintance with the police chief.

"What are the odds the same person who slashed my tires did this, too?"

"It's a possibility we'll take seriously."

Matt sent Art a half smile. Even small-town police played their cases close to the vest.

"I get the sense that the message is a threat toward me, not my dog." He shoved the wiggling animal into the pen and latched the gate. "Sorry, boy. I know you wanted to make a new friend, but I think he'd rather not be slobbered on."

Art chuckled. Ben whined after them as Matt fell into step with the police chief on the sidewalk leading toward the front of the house.

"There's a malicious pettiness about the crazy things happening in Abbottsville," Matt continued. "Even the poisoning. I doubt the culprit expected anyone to die. The point seemed more to make people suffer. He…or she…was probably as shocked by Mr. Clemson's passing as anyone. Maybe more so, because the death took their crime to a whole new level."

Art gave a noncommittal grunt, but his gaze was anything but disinterested. "You sense a connection between the threats toward you and the poison case? Why?"

They stopped next to Art's vehicle, idling at the curb. Matt glared through the window at the envelope of dog hair that sat, bagged and labeled, on the passenger seat.

"I've been a player in this investigation since the beginning, and I'm spending time with Kelly. She and her family are keys in this case, but I haven't figured out the angle yet."

A slow smile spread across the chief's face. "If you ever get tired of chasing germs, you should consider chasing crooks. You think like a cop."

"I'll take that as a high compliment." Matt laughed. "If Greg weren't already in jail, he'd be my chief suspect."

Art frowned. "Guess I'd better tell you about Greg."

"He made bail this morning?" Kelly blinked at Chelsea.

"It's a miracle." The woman beamed. "The bail bondsman received an anonymous cash donation designated for Greg's bail. He gave us a call, and Nick was out the door to pick up his son like his tail was on fire."

"Greg is home?" Kelly stopped walking.

They were in sight of the Miltons' house from the opposite direction in which they'd started. Why hadn't she noticed that the route they were walking would make it necessary for her to pass their place to get back to her car? She eyed the front steps, half expecting the teenager to barrel out the door toward them.

Chelsea had gone suspiciously silent. Kelly gazed down at her.

The woman grimaced. "He's not exactly home. He and his dad started fighting before they got back. As soon as they pulled into the driveway, Greg took off on foot."

"Your son is loose on the town somewhere?"

Chelsea let out a titter. "You make it sound like he's public enemy number one. He's been a good worker for Brenda. He loves that woman like a second mom, and the feeling is mutual. Maybe she's the anonymous donor. I'm not worried about Greg. He'll come home when he gets hungry."

A bellow drew their attention toward the Milton home. A burly figure stood swaying on the top step. The heat of his glare shot icicles through Kelly's insides.

Matt shook his head. "With Greg sprung, we're left with no suspects eliminated."

"That's about the size of it." Art went around to the driver's-side door of his vehicle. "I'll run this envelope to the station, then pay a visit to the Milton house."

Matt watched the police cruiser glide up the street then pulled his cell phone from his pocket. Ben's hair had been shaved to stubble in wide swaths like the tracks an electric shaver would make. He needed to ask Kelly if his dog's skin was in danger of frostbite. At least he could thank the creep who did this for another opportunity to speak to a certain lovely redhead.

Tim picked up on the third ring. The man's greeting was professional but curt.

"I have a question for Kelly," Matt said. "Is she free to come to the phone?"

"She's not here at the moment. May I take a message?"

"Oh." A pregnant pause followed. Uneasiness passed over Matt. "Do you have any idea where she might have gone?"

"I know exactly where she's gone, and if I didn't have to man the fort, I'd go after her."

Dread deepened its grip on Matt. "Feel like sharing?"

"Not really, but somebody's got to save her from her madness. She went to talk to Chelsea Milton. Something set her off, and she feels like she's got to single-handedly solve crime in Abbottsville."

Matt didn't bother to say goodbye as he sprinted to his car.

"I'd better go." Chelsea squeezed Kelly's arm and then gasped.

Kelly followed the waitress's gaze. A husky figure stalked toward the Milton home from another direction. The teenager and his father exchanged curses as the distance closed.

"Oh no they don't! They're not going to start another public scene!" Chelsea released Kelly and began trotting toward her house.

Kelly's gaze traveled from Nick to Greg to Chelsea. A perfect storm was forming before her very eyes, and inserting herself into the mix would only make matters worse. She couldn't stop any action Nick or Greg decided to take and would probably get hurt in the process, while helping no one. The best thing to do was to call the cops—pronto! Unfortunately, she'd left her cell phone in her vehicle. Kelly let out a groan. She'd have to hustle and take a circuitous route that didn't carry her into the thick of the fray forming in the Miltons' front yard.

She turned on her heel and hastily retraced her steps. Up another half block, she found a convenient alley to shorten her trek. The angry voices from the direction of the Miltons' house abruptly cut off. Had hostilities ceased? More likely, Chelsea had shooed her men inside. Who knew what could take place behind closed doors?

Kelly broke into a run. A precious eternity passed—though probably only a minute or two—and then her vehicle finally came into view. While she beelined toward it, she dug in her jacket pocket for her keys. Puffing, she unlocked her door, whipped it open and grabbed her handbag off the front seat.

Bang!

The shot whipped her head around. Her eyes went enormous.

That was no gunshot. It was the Miltons' van backfiring. The sun's glare on the windshield prevented her from seeing who was behind the wheel. But unless they swerved, they were going to hit her.

Her open vehicle door stood between her and a dash for escape. She had a split-second chance to dive headfirst toward the passenger side of her vehicle.

She took her chance.

SEVEN

The screech of agonized metal reached Matt's ears as he neared the final turn onto the Miltons' street. His foot tromped the accelerator, and he skidded around the corner. All was quiet in front of the Miltons' house, but a few blocks away a van sped from the wreckage of a familiar vehicle. Matt's pulse rocketed, and red haze edged his vision.

Seconds dragged as he roared toward Kelly's crippled SUV. That dinosaur of a van was built like a tank. It had swiped the driver's side of the Explorer and ripped the door off. Pieces of metal and glass were strewed on the road. Had Kelly been behind the wheel? Would he find her body in the same shape as her vehicle?

Matt slammed on his brakes and charged from his car before the chassis stopped rocking. "Kelly!" Debris crunched beneath his shoes as he flew toward the Explorer.

Impossibly, wonderfully, the passenger-side door opened, and a flame-haired figure tumbled out and collapsed to her knees. Matt threw himself down beside her. He resisted the urge to squeeze her tight. Not until he assessed the nature of her injuries. She appeared whole, but her green gaze stared through him, unfocused.

"Kelly?"

"Oh, Matt!" She flung herself at him.

He wrapped her close. "I'm here, honey. Everything's going to be all right."

As soon as he throttled the life out of the driver of that van.

Kelly wiggled away. "We have to call the police. They might be dead."

"Who could be dead?"

"I have no idea who left the house in that van, but Chelsea, Nick and Greg were fighting like cats and dogs when they went inside. I'm scared of what might have happened, especially since one of them just tried to kill me."

"I see your point." Matt felt along his belt for his phone, then froze at the blare of a siren almost in his back pocket. He turned his head to see Art's vehicle pull up behind his car. That's right. The chief had intended to pay a visit to the Miltons, anyway.

Art hustled toward them. "What's the story here?"

Matt helped Kelly to her feet, and she swiftly sketched events following a walk in the fresh air with Chelsea. "But that's not all," she finished, "I've discovered a motive Chelsea—or any of the Miltons—might have had to slip poison into the sweet tea at Brenda's Kitchen."

"I'll be asking you about that further." The chief pointed a finger at Kelly. "But first I'm going to call for backup and put out a bulletin on that van." He trotted to his cruiser.

Kelly sagged, and Matt wrapped his arm around her shoulders. He gazed into her pale face. "Looks like you have a goose egg forming on your forehead."

She touched the spot near the part in her hair. "I banged my head on the dashboard when I leapt to get out of the path of the van."

"You don't feel dizzy?"

She shook her head. "Angry. Frightened. Shaky. But not dizzy."

"Let's get into my car."

She allowed him to guide her toward his vehicle with no attempt to release herself from his arm around her shoulder. Good thing. He'd come too close to losing her to let go lightly. Now, his task was to convince her to feel the same way about him. He settled her in the passenger side of his car, then got in behind the wheel.

Color had returned to her face, and her eyes held a steely glint. "What a mess people make of their lives, and for the dumbest reasons. Somebody said something mean about them."

"More battles are fought over words than any other reason."

"Tell me about it. I've come to realize 'idle chatter' like the Simms sisters' isn't very harmless."

A knock sounded on Matt's window, and he powered it down to look into Art's grim face.

"Backup is on the way to secure this accident scene and check on the Milton residence, but I have to leave. They've found the van."

"Where?" The question chorused from Matt and Kelly in unison.

Art heaved a sigh. "Buried in the front of the veterinary clinic."

Tingles, as if she were recovering from numbness, passed across Kelly's skin. Matt's hand found hers and squeezed. She met his concerned gaze.

"Someone rammed my business?" Her words came out breathless, then her spine stiffened. "Tim! He's in there." She looked around, and Art was screeching a U-turn out of his parking spot, lights whirling. She stared at Matt. Why was he sitting there? "Let's go!"

He squinted at her. "Aren't we supposed to remain at the scene of an accident? And when we go anywhere, it should be to the clinic to have that head bump checked out."

"There's been a disaster at my business, and someone I care about may be hurt or…" She couldn't finish the sentence over the lump in her throat. "Go!" she croaked.

"Yes, ma'am." He shook his head but performed a smooth turn and soon had them on the tail of Art's police cruiser.

On the way, they passed a unit headed toward the Miltons' neighborhood. Her gaze followed the black-and-white as it whizzed by, and she prayed for whoever remained in that home. What would the officer find when he gained entrance?

"Hang in there, Kelly." Matt's words were strong and calm. "Tim may be a mope-head, but he's a survivor. He's proven that much."

She sent him a tight smile. This was a good guy to have around in a crisis.

Minutes later, they arrived at the veterinary clinic. Matt pulled the car to the curb across the street, but that was as close as they could get with squad cars and a fire truck filling the clinic parking lot.

Kelly gaped. She had no words. The rear half of the Miltons' van stuck out from her building. The front half was swallowed in what remained of her front door and picture window. The roof had collapsed onto the forward portion of the van, rendering it inaccessible to rescue workers. Power lines that had been attached to the roof corner dangled, sparking, on the ground. Personnel were assessing the scene.

Kelly climbed out of the car.

"Where are you going?" Matt called.

She didn't answer as she headed across the street. Art intercepted her.

"Have they found Tim?" She bounced on the balls of her feet, straining for any view of what was going on, but the fire truck blocked her view.

"If you'll open the rear door, we'll send a crew in to look for him."

The warmth of Matt's presence appeared at Kelly's side. Solid. Comforting. Some of the gelatin in the pit of her stomach ceased quivering.

Another officer and a fireman, bearing flashlights, joined them on their route around the building. Her hand shook as she unlocked the door. She swallowed an impulse to race inside, calling Tim's name. What if she found him, and he wasn't all right? She swallowed a bitter taste. Better to let the professionals handle this part. She stepped back into Matt's waiting arms.

A whine of power tools began out front. Rescue workers must be cutting away debris from around the van. The noise killed conversation. Just as well. If Matt wasn't here holding her up, she'd be a puddle on the ground.

Under other circumstances, holding Kelly Granger would be a dream come true. This felt more like a nightmare. Her frame shuddered in his arms. This woman had absorbed blow after blow in her young life…and now this. Insurance could fix her building, but it couldn't fix her heart if she loved Tim Hallock and lost him. For her sake, Matt prayed with all his heart that Tim would be found alive and well.

Long seconds ticked past. At last, Art and the search party emerged, and Kelly pulled away from Matt. The hungry hope on her face twisted his heart.

The police chief shook his head. "No sign of him."

"But his car is here." She waved toward the compact vehicle.

Art's flat gaze locked with Matt's. Unless Tim had stepped out for something, they both knew that under the wreckage was the likely place to find him—along with the driver of the van. Was that driver also the person responsible for putting the mistletoe in the tea? The conclusion didn't require a leap of genius. Matt lifted his chin, and Art returned a tiny nod.

The chief's attention went to Kelly. "We took a peek into the front room, but the only safe way to approach clearing the debris is from the outside. More of the roof could collapse at any time. If you two want to be of help, lock this door and then go find a warm place to pray."

"Sounds like a plan," Matt said.

Art and his men hustled off. Kelly stood frozen, gazing after them.

"Let me take you somewhere for a hot coffee. From there,

we can call Brenda as well as people from your church, if you'd like, to enlist more prayers." He offered a gentle smile.

A long breath escaped her lips. "Thank you. You're a good man."

Matt's heart sank further, if that were possible, but he held his smile in place. Those were the words a woman said to a man she regarded as nothing more than a friend. He held out his hand, but she turned away and opened the clinic door.

"Where do you think you're going?" He stepped into her path. "Didn't you hear the chief? It's dangerous in there."

She glared up at him, hands on hips. An impossible jolt of attraction shot through him—a reaction he was going to have to learn to overcome. Or move to another town—again.

"Matthew Bennett, I have patients in there. About now, they're scared out of their wits, and if more of the roof is about to fall, I need to get them out."

"Correction. *We* need to get them out."

He propped the door open with a sliver of wood that looked as if that were its function. With the power cut to the building, they'd need any daylight they could get.

"Like I said. You're a good man." She tapped his shoulder as she breezed past him and led the way to the convalescent room.

Plaintive mewing and whining carried above the cacophony from the rescue workers outside, but the animal cages were a dim outline in this windowless room.

"There's a flashlight in a drawer," Kelly said.

She headed for a bank of cabinets on one wall, and Matt stayed close behind. Suddenly an out-of-place sound arrested him. Did he hear what he thought he heard? A human groan? He started to turn, but pain exploded in his head.

Once. Then again. Then blackness.

"Matt?" The sudden loss of his presence was tangible.

Kelly turned. He wasn't standing behind her. She gazed

around, eyes adjusting to the dimness, and found his form sprawled headlong on the floor. What had happened?

A beam of light speared the darkness, and Kelly shaded her eyes with her forearm. A dark silhouette held the flashlight she'd been looking for. The person's other hand pointed a much different object in her direction.

Kelly's mouth went dry. Did this creep's repertoire never end? Poison, a knife and now a gun.

"Couldn't you this once have played the helpless bystander?" Tones of disgust came from behind the light. "Now my plans need to change drastically again."

Kelly's heart did a somersault. She knew that voice, but couldn't believe her ears.

EIGHT

"Tim! You're all right. I was afraid they'd find you under the wreckage. What are you doing with a gun? I'm no threat to you."

"You've always been a threat."

"What are you talking about?"

"Always looking out for poor Tim. Championing me to the public." A sneer tainted his voice. "Don't you know that was the last straw with Hayley that proved the Simms sisters' whispers to the community grapevine that I was stepping out on her? With you!"

Kelly's lungs constricted. "That's nonsense! I never heard such a rumor."

"Typical for the object of gossip to be the last to hear. Don't worry. I don't blame you. I never did. You were being your usual, decent self. Someone else putting a sick spin on your actions never occurred to you. Frankly, I don't think many people took stock in *us* as a twosome except Hayley, but it gave her one more excuse to leave me."

Thoughts tumbled through Kelly's brain, and a few bits clicked together. "*You* put the Iscador in the sweet tea to get back at the Simms sisters!"

"Partially accurate. The sisters were prime targets, but so were any of the coffee-klatch clan at Brenda's Kitchen. That bunch of vicious gossips had a bellyache coming."

A rock weighted the pit of Kelly's stomach. She'd trusted

this man. Admired his faithfulness. Defended him when no one else would. And now, she saw with 20/20 hindsight that his chronic depression formed the outer layer around more sinister mental problems.

"Did Mr. Clemson have an early grave coming?"

Tim's hiss of indrawn breath indicated her words had scored a hit. "How was I to know somebody's ticker would give out over a touch of illness not much worse than the stomach flu? And you're wrong on an important point. I did *not* put the Iscador in the tea."

"But you stole it from my sister's house during the Christmas party. I should have guessed the culprit was someone with medical training." Kelly paused, then gasped. "The drug used to knock me out when I came to the clinic! You knew what it was and what it would do. Did you supply it to whoever grabbed me? But if you were involved in the vandalism at the clinic, why were you unconscious on the floor? Did you stage that as part of the cover-up for the theft of the biological samples? Did you poison the pets, too?"

"Shut! Up!" The gun's aim zeroed in on her heart. "I would never, ever hurt a defenseless animal, but when you work with an idiot bad things happen."

Kelly's pulse raced. "Idiot?"

A groan from the darkness followed on the heels of her question.

Tim darted the flashlight beam toward the open utility closet. A bulky form hunched on the floor against the wall. His head hung, and dark stains on his clothing suggested blood.

"Nick Milton," Kelly breathed. "*He* put the poison in the tea."

The man had a bad habit of barging into the kitchen when his wife was working. No one would have remarked the occurrence as unusual, any more than the oft-repeated kerfuffle of Brenda tossing him out.

"Bingo!" Tim said. "No persuasion was necessary to enlist his help in doing this community a little dirt…except the fool got carried away. He went on a spree of feeding poisoned hamburger to people's pets."

"But why did he almost run me down in his van this afternoon? And why ram the clinic?"

"Cross-eyed drunk. He probably had no idea you were in his way. I was his target after I informed him on the phone that the bail money for his son was the only payment for the tea caper he was going to get from me. When he hurt the animals, he forfeited the rest of the money I promised for the job."

"So nobody is under the wreckage out front that our firefighters and police force are risking themselves to search?"

"The project keeps them out of our way, doesn't it?" Tim laughed. "It took a minute or so for the roof to fall in. The old sot got out of his vehicle just in time. I hauled him into the closet, and we both waited out the official search for good old Tim. I knew they'd never check the closet during a scour of the premises designed to locate someone they assumed *wanted* to be found. It would be easy for me to claim later that Nick held me quiet at gunpoint. When everyone cleared out, Nick and I were going to have a fight for survival, and he was going to take a bullet while I emerged the town hero for single-handedly taking down the murderer. But then you and Mr. Noble had to bust in on the party." He nudged Matt's inert form with his foot.

The beam of the flashlight returned to Kelly's face. She winced at the brightness but refused to look away. "Don't do this, Tim. There's help for you. We'll get some. I promise."

Click!

The cocking of the gun resounded in her ears, even over the noise the rescuers were making outside. The breath stalled in her throat.

"Quit patronizing me! There was a time after Hayley left me that I considered making a play for you—turning those rumors into truth. But I could see there was no use in it. You regarded me as another wounded creature to fix. Did it ever occur to your self-righteous mind that I don't want to be fixed?"

Kelly's hands fisted. There was no chance she could reach Tim before he shot her, but she wasn't going down easy. How horrible that Matt should lose his life because of her. The man had made himself precious to her in a short period of time.

"I'm afraid my simple scenario will have to become more complicated," Tim went on. "Nick is going to shoot you and Matt, and then he and I will wrestle for control of the gun. I'll win, of course, and still emerge the town hero—a tragic one, which is even more sympathetic—because I will have lost my beloved boss in the dramatic scuffle. And a state employee will be dead. The whole thing will make the news! Hayley's going to hear what kind of man her ex has turned out to be and wish she'd never left."

Tim's too-bright cackle raised the hairs on the nape of Kelly's neck.

"It's been nice knowing you," he said. "I mean that. But now it's bye-bye."

Kelly steeled herself to leap. Sudden movement halted her. Matt's arm swept Tim's feet from under him. The gun exploded, and a mosquito whine zipped past Kelly's ear. A ceiling tile burst in a puff of debris that rained on her head and stung her eyes. She screamed and scrubbed frantically at her face, but her blurred vision offered a skewed picture of the men wrestling on the linoleum. Through the tangle of arms and legs, she could barely tell which dark figure was Matt and which was Tim. Matt was bigger and stronger, but he'd taken a blow to the head. Tim was wiry and fueled by madness. Grunts and yelps punctuated their struggle.

Where was the gun?

A second shot chilled her bones and shattered glass somewhere in the room. The men were fighting for possession of it.

The flashlight had rolled away and rested by the wall. Kelly scurried to retrieve it. She could use it to clobber Tim—if the men held still long enough. She whirled and pointed the light at the combatants as the gun discharged again. The explosion sent tremors to her core.

Both men went limp and lay still, Tim sprawled on top. Matt's eyes were closed, his face slack. A thread of blood began to creep across the linoleum toward Kelly.

Horror constricted her throat. "Matt?"

One man stirred. The other did not respond.

All strength left Kelly's knees. She buckled to the floor, tears hot on her cheeks.

NINE

Matt accepted the cup of cocoa Kelly held toward him and relaxed into the comfort of an easy chair in her living room. Ben snoozed on the floor at his feet.

Kelly hovered over him. "Can I get you anything else? A sandwich, maybe?"

"Thank you, but a sandwich is the last thing on my wish list." He smiled up at her. How did this woman grow more beautiful every time he saw her?

A furrow appeared between her brows. "Are you all right? Does your head bother you?"

"I'm fine. Really." He touched the bandage that covered the spot where Tim had clobbered him.

For a scrawny fellow, the guy had a batter's arm. If Matt's head had been a baseball, it would have been out of the park. Kelly had just brought him home after three days in the hospital, recuperating from a concussion. It was by the pure grace of God that he'd roused that day at the clinic and found the strength to stop Tim from putting bullets into them both, before passing out again. But he'd repeat the agony, and lots worse, to hang on to that special glow in Kelly's eyes when she gazed at him. Did he dare hope that look was telling him things he longed to hear?

"Okay." She didn't sound convinced. "The way you were staring at me, I wasn't sure."

"Frankly, looking at you is my best therapy right now."

Her cheeks went pink. "I'm so thankful you're all right. I don't know what I would have done if…" Her words trailed off, and she bit her bottom lip.

Matt set his cocoa on the side table and rose. The room did a little wobble—residual effects from his head blow—but he couldn't bear to delay this moment any longer.

"Kelly." He cupped her shoulders in his hands. "We've been through a lot in the past couple of weeks. Our emotions have been all over the place. But I know one thing. From that first meeting, when you looked at me with gorgeous fire in your eyes, I started falling hard and fast. I don't want to be your friend…or even the guy who saved your life. I was saving my own, too, by the way, so you don't owe me sandwiches or cocoa or hand-and-foot service. I don't want your gratitude. I want to win your heart. Do I stand a chance?"

Her emerald gaze sparked. "Matthew Bennett, do you honestly expect me to fall in love with you?"

His gut twisted, but he forced a brave face. "A man can always hope."

A slow smile tilted the corners of her lips, and her arms slid around his neck. "That he can! And sometimes hope is rewarded."

Heart beating a tattoo against his ribs, Matt gathered her warmth close and lowered his head toward her upturned face, and—the doorbell rang, loud and long. They groaned in unison.

"You don't have to answer," Matt suggested, not loosening his hold.

The bell sounded again in several short jabs. Ben leaped up and barked.

Huffing, Kelly wriggled away from him. He released her, mentally smacking the intruder on the doorstep. She went toward the foyer, his dog at her heels. Moments later, she and Ben returned with Art in tow. The man had the gall to grin and clap Matt on the shoulder. Then he plopped onto the couch, looking like he planned to stay awhile.

"I'll grab you a cup of coffee," Kelly said to their visitor.

"Thanks." Art nodded. "I could use one of those."

The heavy-lidded glance Kelly shot Matt's direction sent his pulse into overdrive. Then she exited toward the kitchen. What might the penalty be for tossing the chief of police out onto the lawn...if he could muster the strength to do it?

"How are you feeling today, young man?"

Matt's gaze returned to Art and found the chief staring at him like a specimen under a microscope. Scrapping thoughts of mayhem, Matt offered a rueful smile. "I don't feel quite so much like I've been run over by a semi. Just stomped by a mad bull."

Art chuckled. "You slept so long and hard, we were beginning to think you planned to hibernate for the rest of the winter."

Ben ambled over to the newcomer, sniffing but not leaping and jumping. Art began to scratch the animal's head, and Ben plopped onto his haunches in canine bliss. Matt's brows lifted. His dog was already behaving more civilized since Kelly had been looking after him while he was in the hospital.

"Mind telling me what you remember from events at the clinic?" the chief asked.

"I'll tell you what I can, but my last clear memory is you reporting to us outside the clinic that there was no sign of Tim. After that, it's piecemeal."

"Normal for a head blow. Kelly is clear on everything, so whatever you can contribute will merely corroborate."

In a few short sentences, Matt recounted awakening on the floor of the clinic to hear Tim about to shoot Kelly and then wrestling with the madman until Tim was accidentally shot and went limp. Then Matt passed out again.

"Maybe you can connect a few dots for me," he said to Art. "Did I imagine it, or was Nick Milton at the clinic, too? And what happened to Chelsea and Greg?"

"You weren't imagining things. When my officer arrived at the Milton place, he found it empty. Turns out Chelsea and

Greg had fled for their lives out the side door. They showed up later, hale and healthy. Ramming the clinic cost Nick broken bones, cuts and abrasions, but like Tim, he'll recover to answer for his crimes."

Matt let out a long breath. "Tim survived his gunshot wound then. I'm relieved I didn't kill someone, even if he *was* trying to kill *us*."

Art shook his head. "That guy is more likely to see the inside of a looney bin than a prison. He's lost it! Raves delusional nonsense, nonstop, about his ex-wife and being her hero. But his babbling has filled in a few factual blanks for us, too."

Kelly returned with a steaming cup, which she handed to Art, and then took a seat in the easy chair opposite Matt.

"I'm heartbroken about Tim," she said. "It's hard for me to wrap my head around the idea that he not only tried to kill Matt and me, but he's the one who trashed the clinic to make it look like a break-in. Then he grabbed me and knocked me out with that sedative when I arrived at work earlier than he expected."

"There was method to his madness." Art grimaced. "The back door was standing wide open when Matt arrived that morning, because Tim was about to cart away a few pieces of valuable equipment so the missing biological samples wouldn't look so suspicious. He tossed those into the woods out back. We found them once we had an idea where to look."

Matt looked from Art to Kelly and back again. "Tim was the sole culprit who staged the clinic break-in? How did he end up knocked out with a head gash?"

"You'll hardly believe this." Art slapped his knee. "Goes to show how nuts he is. But when he heard you enter the clinic, he bonked himself on the head with the flashlight, hid it under the flooring of an empty animal cage and then sprawled out for you and Kelly to find. He never was unconscious. Not at all the scenario he had planned. He'd intended to put on a show as if he'd fought off a masked intruder and rescued Kelly, but then you turned up and hogged the glory instead. He hated your guts after that and put Nick up to doing whatever dirt he could to you."

A sour taste settled on Matt's tongue. He took a sip of sweet hot chocolate. People resorted to the most outrageous actions for the most ridiculous reasons. "Nick is the one who slashed my tires and shaved my dog?" He clucked to Ben, and the animal trotted over and placed his head on Matt's knees. He ruffled the fur behind the Saint Bernard's ears.

"Nick doesn't admit to anything," Art said. "However, we're confident that the fibers found in the knife hilt will match a pair of his gloves, and we found dog hair in his electric shaver, so his goose is well-done on those charges. But the guy's got bigger legal concerns. Which reminds me—" he laid his coffee cup aside "—there are a ton of reports on my office desk that need filing."

He rose and Matt started to get up, but Art motioned him to remain seated—Kelly, too. "I'll let you folks get back to whatever you were doing." He shot them a broad wink and exited, chuckling.

Matt caught Kelly's eye. She turned bright red, then they both laughed. Matt held out his arms, and she glided over to him. He tugged her hands, and she settled gingerly on his lap.

"Am I hurting you?"

"My head is probably going to ache for a while, but my heart will hurt worse if I can't finally kiss you like I've dreamed of doing."

"Whatever shall I think of such a forward neighbor?" She laid a finger to her chin, and her sparkling eyes teased him.

"Do you want me to hunt up some mistletoe so we can put it to its proper use?"

Kelly made a face then grinned at him. "Why wait for mistletoe?"

She lowered her head toward his, and their lips met in a lingering kiss which promised many more to come.

Kelly rested with her head on Matt's broad shoulder. When was the last time she'd felt so safe, accepted and loved? Too long. This was not the kind of man who left a girl for the glitter of gold and the promise of prestige. She could see them together for the long haul, probably in his larger house next door—big Ben acting the furry nanny to their kids. Saint Bernards were notoriously protective.

She hated to disturb this dreamy moment with a touchy subject, but she wanted Matt to be aware of her decision before she filed the paperwork. The issue involved him, too. Lifting her head, she met his deep blue gaze. Happiness glowed from him.

"What's on your mind, sweetheart?" he asked. "I can see those wheels turning."

She exhaled a long breath. "You're good. Evidently, we're embarking on a transparent relationship. I like that…I think." She tweaked a lock of the fair hair on his forehead.

He grinned. "I agree, and I'm all ears."

She rose from her comfortable perch on his lap and went to a small writing desk in the corner of the room. The letter with the return address of the county courthouse lay on top of a short stack of mail. She gave the envelope to Matt, then settled in the easy chair opposite his while he read the letter.

Shortly, he lifted his gaze from the paper, brow furrowed. "Let me see if I understand. As one of the victims of Greg's assault, the judge wants you to submit a written recommendation of what you feel the boy's consequences should be?"

"The request is common in these cases. It doesn't mean the judge will abide by my recommendation, but he will consider my opinion."

Matt snorted. "Ship the kid to juvenile hall. He's a menace."

"I understand your feelings, but I need to fill out the story for you. Obviously, Greg hasn't had it easy at home, and his rough exterior hasn't made him popular at school. Brutus was his only friend—other than his mother. Losing the dog made his pain unbearable."

"So it's okay that he came after you?" Matt scowled. "It's not all right with me."

Kelly took a deep breath. He was going all protective on her, exactly as she'd expected. A part of her liked the reaction; another part dreaded his response to her plan of action.

"Did you know Greg saved Ben?" She pronounced the words softly but clearly.

"He what?"

"After Nick picked Greg up from jail, the man was bent on getting back at you for your part in putting his son behind bars. He thought Greg would go along with his plan to hurt Ben, but the kid threw such a fit that Nick settled for shaving Ben instead of cutting him."

"Nick was going to cut my dog?" Matt sat bolt upright, then moaned and pressed a palm to his forehead.

Ben whined, probably from Matt's tone. Kelly crossed the room and settled one hand on Matt's tense shoulder while scratching behind Ben's ear with the other.

"Take it easy, you two. It didn't happen." She stared into Matt's eyes. "And you have Greg to thank. That's what father and son were fighting about when they arrived home from their pit stop at your house. You know the rest of that story."

Matt sighed and closed his eyes. His Adam's apple bobbed a couple of times then he squinted up at her. "So you're going to tell the judge to go easy on Greg?"

"Not exactly." Kelly settled herself onto a place that was rapidly becoming her favorite perch—Matt's lap. "Brutus has been approved by the Humane Society for reeducation. Since Nick Milton is going to be out of the home for a long time, I believe Greg should be sentenced to taking that rehabilitation training with his dog, and that Brutus should be restored to Greg's custody if they both successfully complete the course. A class like that teaches the owner as much self-control and responsibility as it does the animal."

A smile formed on Matt's lips. "You are one amazing lady!"

Kelly's insides warmed. "You're not angry?"

"Not any longer." His arms tightened around her, and Kelly snuggled closer.

"One more thing before we resume getting better acquainted." She tapped the end of his nose with her finger. "Greg claims his dad must have been the one who turned Brutus loose on me. He says Nick wasn't passed out drunk that afternoon."

"So the lout was putting on a show for Art and me?"

"Apparently. But we can't prove it."

Matt frowned. "I'm not happy about him getting away with anything, but like Art says, the guy has bigger legal concerns."

"I'm happy to let the system handle Nick Milton. I should have guessed he was behind the pet poisonings when his dog was the only one brought in that day with no illness."

"Don't beat yourself up because you're a decent person and it didn't occur to you to suspect that someone was poisoning animals on purpose. Say! How is your sister doing now that she can reopen her business?"

Kelly laughed. "Brenda's busier than a fly on a Christmas fruit cake. After all the notoriety, and now that the poisoner is caught, people are streaming in from out of town to try the fare and loving it. Chelsea is happy working double shifts. Not just because they can use the money, but it keeps her mind off her family woes. She may be the only person in town who's sad about Nick's arrest."

"That leaves one burning question." Matt lifted a brow.

Kelly held her breath.

"When are you going to start training Ben and me?"

Kelly exhaled a chuckle. "We'll get serious as soon as you're able to walk, trot and jog without falling over."

Matt grinned. "I like the idea of getting serious."

Kelly matched his grin. "I believe this is going to be a wonderful Christmas after all."

EPILOGUE

One Year Later

"I now pronounce you husband and wife." The pastor beamed at the newlyweds.

Kelly's heart swelled as she gazed into Matt's ardent eyes. His triumphant grin outshone the pastor's. She suppressed the urge to bounce on the balls of feet clad in white, organdy slippers. They held hands beneath an archway adorned with bright red and pure white poinsettias and sprinkled with holly sprigs in honor of the Christmas season. Not a trace of mistletoe, but she didn't need an herb to tell her when to kiss the man she loved.

When was the minister going to say it?

A pregnant pause spread a hush across the guests packed into the cozy church.

"You may kiss the bride," the pastor intoned.

Finally!

Kelly melted into her new husband's arms and sealed their union with a tender savor of his lips. The guests erupted into glad applause, and her heart lifted toward God in praise.

Last Christmas had turned out wonderful after the danger had passed, but this one outstripped them all.

* * * * *

Dear Reader,

Matt and Kelly's story is dear to my heart. The writing of it enriched my own life with illumination in sensitive areas of our human condition.

The tale serves as a tribute to all those who have fought and are still fighting the battle of breast cancer, as well as the family and friends who stand with them. A coworker of mine fought the fight and remains with us, but those who have passed from this life knowing Christ have entered into the ultimate victory.

This story is also an illustration of the power of words—for good or ill. How lightly we sometimes speak when we ought to weigh our words!

Matt and Kelly's budding romance demonstrates triumph over loss and the gift of a second chance at love. How often do we guard our hearts against new opportunities for relationships because of the memory of old losses and hurts? Each day is new in the Lord. Let us say with Paul, "Forgetting what is behind and straining toward what is ahead, I press on toward the goal..." Philippians 3:31b—14a. (*New International Version*)

I hope you found pleasure and blessing in the read. Please drop by and visit me at http://www.jillelizabethnelson.com.

In Him,
Jill Elizabeth Nelson

Questions for Discussion

1. At the end of the first scene, Kelly is upset with Matt. Is her anger about the loss of her decorations, or is there a deeper reason? If so, what is it?

2. Matt moves to Abbottsville seeking a haven. He finds the opposite. How often do we take an action in order to gain one thing but end up with something different? Can this result be the plan of God? Discuss.

3. Brenda's response to tragedy is silence. How do you process shocks? Are you prone to inward contemplation or outward venting? Is one response healthier than the other?

4. Why does Brenda have a calm, practical perspective on Matt's role in her restaurant closing, while Kelly takes his actions personally?

5. Who does Kelly feel Matt resembles, not physically but in his character, that creates a strong attraction for her? Do we often seek qualities in a mate that are familiar to us from our upbringing? How can this work in a healthy way? How might this be unhealthy?

6. Gossip is a rampant evil, even among those who claim the name of Christ. Have you ever been stuck in an uncomfortable situation where someone insisted upon sharing the latest juicy tidbit about someone else, along with surmising and assumptions? How did you handle the situation? Have *you* ever been guilty of gossip?

7. Do you agree with Matt's statement that our attitude invites matching events into our lives? Why or why not?

"Above all else, guard your heart, for it is the well-spring of life." Proverbs 4:24. What does this mean?

8. The severe dysfunction in the Milton family is all too common. Matt isn't inclined toward compassion. Why? And why is Kelly? How does a Christian balance compassion for souls in misery with the need for justice, as well as protection for the people they may hurt?